If you seek Love

And are a lover of Love

Take a sharp knife in your hand

And slit the throat of self-restraint

—JALALUDDIN RUMI

# Chapter One

On a usual, slow night in mid-September, 1964, Charlie Dyer came to the Beach Cart grocery store located half way out on Longboat Key, an island shaped like a sleeping eel, off of Sarasota, Florida.

"I'm not looking for groceries, I'm lookin' for work," Charlie said to John Spradlin, age 22 lone clerk, indeed, lone person in the store.

"Jimmy's not here now. He goes home at 6:30."

"Who's Jimmy?"

"The owner. He does the hiring."

"I suppose he hired you."

"Yes, he did."

"And probably a wise move on his part, don't you think?"

Spradlin only smiled, wondering why such an old codger was trying to bait him. Spradlin studied Dyer's khaki shorts and his knobby near bow legs, studded with wiry grey blond hair, finally said, "You could try tomorrow. He's here from 8:30 to 6:30 every day."

"You're a kind lad," Dyer said. "But at my age I don't plan tomorrows, and I don't buy green bananas."

"I bet you do, if they're cheap enough."

"Shedding your kindness already? Happens a lot with me. People don't like the way I talk directly. For example, if I'm going to be with a woman, I always take a shower first. Always."

"That's good." Spradlin said. "But I bet you haven't showered in quite a while."

Dyer laughed. "You seem lively for a clerk at a place like this." Dyer nodded toward the wall board already water stained and sagging, nodded toward the overhead metal grid work that supported the sagging tin roof already studded with hanging pails to catch rain leaks. "You related to Jimmy? I figure somebody with your tongue has to be part of the ownership of this place."

"No."

"Oh come on! You could own up to it. I'm not a threat to anyone. Just lookin' for work. You think Jimmy'd hire me? Does he hate old people?"

"He might not like you much, but he did mention he needed help in the day time."

Dyer's eyes danced a short bit. "You give an old duffer like me a reason to come back in the morning. And that's a tankful."

"So come back, and I'll show how to work here," Spradlin said.

"Sonny, I doubt you could show me anything."

In the morning Spradlin opened the store, then went back to his car, a yellow 1956 Plymouth coup, to bring in the cash drawer. He toweled off the moisture on the front glass doors and thought once more about getting a tall stool to sit on near the cash register, but he remembered Jimmy's soft-spoken threat: "You sit down and pretty soon you're doing a sitting-down kind of business. So don't sit down."

At 9:30 Charlie Dyer came in and Spradlin said, "Jimmy's not here. He's sick."

Dyer frowned and then looked skeptical.

"But," Spradlin continued, "he said you could clean up the meat counter and Earl's station before he comes in at noon. Jimmy'l pay you a going wage, whatever that is."

"I wonder what that is," Dyer said.

"Jimmy's fair," Spradlin said. "He said I should show you what needs to be done."

"How lucky is that?"

"Pretty damn lucky, I think."

"You'll see I'm a good worker. Fast, and kind, and well spoken."

"Earl won't care."

"But I'll wager Jimmy will."

"We could argue about that, or I could show you what needs to be done."

Spradlin took him to the back of the store, to the ten foot space behind Earl's meat display counter. He gave him a large stainless steel scrapper and showed him how to clear the surface of the tall butcher block station for carving, how to spread fresh sawdust in front of the case, indicated where rags were kept to wipe clean the glass front of Earl's counter.

"Take your time, "Spradlin said, "Earl's mean and particular."

"How mean?"

"Just listen carefully to Earl and do what he says. Don't give him any lip, on pain of disfigurement."

"Nicely said," Dyer answered.

"Just pay attention." And Spradlin would have elaborated, was in fact looking forward to commenting on the strength of Earl's hooded, angry eyes and tattooed forearms, but the day's first customer came in and Dyer responded as if receiving a stimulant injection. He quickly put on one of Earl's oversize aprons, lapping an extra fold over the rope belt, and hurried to the front of the store.

Spradlin thought Dyer looked ridiculous since his hairy legs extended beyond Earl's folded apron, and Dyer wore mustard-colored old socks that showed above his stained high top sneakers.

"Oh welcome, madam," Dyer shouted. "You're our first customer and you know what they say about the rest of the day resting on the nature of the first transaction. Not that your position in the queue, so to speak, ever would determine our delight in serving you, but, still, the first transaction can set the tone for the rest of the day, the week, the month, the year. Don't you agree?"

The first customer of the day, Clementine Peverill, 74 years old, with silver tinted, close-cropped hair, smiled and said, "John, who is this person, who has so charmed my heart?"

"Charlie Dyer, Jimmy just hired him," Spradlin said, slipping into his post beside the bronze cash register. "He's just started this morning. Say the word and Jimmy will let him go immediately."

"No, never," she said, half laughing, "he's the first ray of sunshine the Beach Cart has had since I don't know when."

"That's me all right, a ray of sunshine, come to brighten up the life of this radiant creature already on fire to sample the world beyond the Beach Cart." Dyer said, offering to push Clementine's somewhat rusty tiny cart. "These are scheduled for an upgrade. Jimmy, himself, told me that this morning, before he got sick."

"Jimmy's sick?" she said, "That's serious. This place can't last a week without Jimmy."

"Oh, yes it can. John and I will see to that, and with customers like you, how could we fail? How could we?"

"You are shameless," she observed. "But I love it. No one talks to me now that Harry's passed."

"I'm sorry to hear that," Dyer said. "Is it recent?"

"Five months and three days tonight by 8:15 p.m."

"At night it was, was it? Better at sunset than sunrise, or so they say. Do you believe it?"

"I'll believe whatever you tell me, or Jimmy tells me, or John says it's so."

"It's always so, if you're alert to it, isn't that so?" Dyer said. "And may I help you with these groceries to your car?"

Clementine laughed. "Not to my car, but to my simple home."

Dyer looked confused.

"My home across the street." She pointed to a cement block ranch style house directly across Gulf of Mexico Drive. The house gave off a fresh pink color, as if white-washed over a maroon primer, in some not recent year. "It's so empty without Harry. And I would be delighted if you would walk me over, after I've made a few selections."

Dyer said, "I've found that a little color banishes memories." He waited to see how she received those remarks and took delight in her smiling thoughtful work-through of his sentiment.

"I should do my work around Earl's counter, while you make your careful purchases. And when you want help just call out. I'll be there in a flash. In a bright blue flash."

Twenty minutes later, when they on the sparse finely broken shells of the Beach Cart's driveway/parking area, she said, "I wonder what color would serve memory best?"

"The man or woman with the Blue Guitar."

"What blue guitar?"

"Oh, things are changed upon the blue guitar. They are, you know. They surely are."

"For me or for Harry?"

"Oh, not extensively for Harry, who's not here, but for you both, sweet madam, in not quite mourning, this morning."

"It's true, I don't mourn."

"But you mope on your blue guitar."

"I do mope. You've got that affixed."

Dyer followed her slowly pushing the nearly empty cart across Gulf of Mexico Drive.

She said, "During tourist season we surely couldn't do this. And I don't want to take you from your work."

"Earl's not in till noon, and besides, he doesn't even know I was hired to clean his space. So there's no loss all the way around. I'm through for Earl."

"Am I just 'no loss?'"

"I am at a loss for words around you. We can shed decades together." Dyer said.

"Wouldn't that be lovely!"

"Madam as surely as God made lawns green, it would. We could take this cart and gallivant down the length of the beach to Longboat's end."

"Which end?"

"Not the Anna Maria end."

"Harry always wanted me to see the St. Armands end, the jungle and the abortive hotel."

"I knew the place," Dyer said. "But you could show me, unless, of course, Earl prevented it."

"But if you don't go back, Earl can't prevent you, can he?" Clementine said with a quick darting eye and all too brief smile.

"Madam we see eye to eye. Perhaps cheek to cheek?"

"Let's take a stroll and see." She answered. "My close friends get to call me 'Tine' and so do you, if you want."

"I want to more than anything on this island."

"I should think the whole wide world."

"Oh, Tine, that too. Of course, that too."

Dyer left the cart in the empty car port, then came back to the front door with its giant silver knocker. She fumbled with the key, but at length she pushed the door back. "I lock since Harry passed," she said.

Three times Dyer brought things in from the cart.

"You are a good worker."

"The best. Always on time and properly dressed. Clean and courteous."

"Oh, that you are. Would you like to hold Puffy," she pointed to a snow-white cat on a snow-white leather couch.

"Not much, I'm afraid of rabies."

"That's silly. Puffy never goes out."

"She'd go out plenty, if I lived here."

"So you do a have a mean streak? I would never have thought so."

"Mean as a snake when the occasion calls for it, mean as a snake."

"We don't have such occasions, do we Mr. Dyer?"

"Not one so far, and that's a good sign."

## 2

That night, Spradlin brought the cash drawer back to Jimmy Faneuf and explained the day, as usual and slow in September. He told Jimmy about Dyer walking Tine home and helping her put away her groceries. Jimmy set aside his fever and followed closely what Spradlin said.

"You know he's short and kind of bow-legged, not the sort Tine Peverill would like, I should think," Spradlin said. "But energetic and eager to please, and withal an engaging personality."

"He comes from tough circumstances," Jimmy said, surprising Spradlin. "Dyers' had a farm outside of Tampa and never did well. Lost the farm, twenty five years ago and Marge never got over that. Ted simply died. And that solved insolvency—pay attention to that."

"Why?"

"If you're dead, your debts are somebody else's problem. Or the debts die with you."

"Okay. If Charlie comes back around, you want to hire him?"

"Yes. Did he come back after taking Tine's groceries over to her place?"

"No."

"Figures. He'll be good for business."

"I don't follow."

"That's why you're not the owner."

"I don't want to be the owner. I want to be a doctor."

"We all have our dreams. Ownership is better than doctoring. Gives you distance."

Jimmy stood up from the rattan couch and tightened the belt of his thin yellow robe. He scratched his head and said, "You know around 2:30 p.m., I sweat like a pig and thought for sure I'd fought off this bug, but all of sudden the fever's back and a kind of sour nausea taste in my throat. The kind of feeling that hopes you could throw up but knows you won't. Earl come in?"

"Yes, on time too. And not pleased with the half-job Charlie did cleaning up. Tine distracted him and I think he spent the afternoon over there, or maybe they went somewhere."

"Oh they went somewhere all right, but slowly with Charlie Dyer talking and talking and Tine listening and listening and feeling suddenly completed again, I bet that happened." Jimmy said. "And if Earl's upset, that's what upset him. Earl has eyes for Tine."

"That's ridiculous. He's not her type at all."

"I understand there's no reciprocation, but what does that mean? Earl has eyes for Tine, calculating eyes. Dyer is more her type—is that what you think?"

"That's what she said. Amazed me, but that's what she said, what she indicated, if you can believe it. I don't, didn't, wouldn't. It's too weird for me."

"Earl will be hurt, but he'll find a way to get past it."

"By chopping up Charlie Dyer."

"That's a possibility," Jimmy said, getting up and tightening his robe. "But we won't have a role in it. Do you believe that?"

"Of course!"

"So let's leave the new couple alone. How old do you think Charlie is?'

"I don't know."

"Of course you don't know and can't even guess. The world looks young to you, John Spradlin. Dyer's 76 and Tine is 74, so there is chemistry even at advanced age. Slow activation time however, slow to mix toward combustion. Slow to ferment into great wine." Jimmy chuckled mostly to himself. He went to the refrigerator. "There's half a sandwich. Cream cheese and olive, left over from supper. You want it?"

"Yes, that's good. I like cream cheese and olive. Maybe they went swimming. Old folks in the sea?"

"They didn't swim. But they talked about it. Doubtless they worried about Red Tide."

"I bet Charlie Dyer is impervious to Red Tide."

"If anybody should be, it would be him. But I bet they didn't say much about it. Too wrapped up in their excitement together. Probably."

"I like the way you know things about people. Or at least you seem to tell clear stories about what they're up to." John Spradlin said.

"Yes," Jimmy answered handing him the half sandwich. "Here's how it went with them. When the groceries were safely away, Charlie suggested they take a stroll on the beach. But Tine said she needed some warm tea before attempting anything, so she sat him down at the glass topped dining table in the nook near the kitchen and watched him look at the white wrought iron curly cues holding the glass in place. After a calculated moment, Charlie brought up Harry's loss, since he figured that was the way to her heart and interest. Charlie asked what kind of a man was he? What were his foibles and which one did she miss

most? Did he suffer at the end? Or was it quick and appropriate, responding to her own needs rather than his? She listened
and checked off as he asked what sort of character Charlie Dyer
was for posing such questions. Each time he passed her tests,
and as a result she didn't steep the tea as long as she had with
Harry. Dyer deserved a lighter brew, and she knew she did too.
Time for a lighter, looser brew with a citrus sharpness and acrid
loosening of grief suddenly found old and unworthy. All in the
brightness off the Gulf through the immense sliding glass doors
of the tiny house's southwest exposure."

## 3.

"The tea was superb but we should walk it off, don't you agree?
A stroll down to St. Armands and perhaps a light lunch, something Mediterranean . . ."

"Oh, Mr. Dyer, let's just sit a while and think about how the
walk would help us, but toward what helpful end?"

"Everyone just calls me Charlie. I'd like you too."

"Doesn't seem special enough, not careful or respectful
enough."

"I don't ever quite get much of that, it's true."

"And it doesn't worry you, does it?"

"If you say so, madam."

"I just see it in the way you look at me. The way you listen
to me. You seem to know who you are, Charlie Dyer. And that's
wonderful. Lately I've not been so sure who I am."

"Happens when a long term partner passes," Dyer said.
"But you pop out of it. Indeed!"

"I like your confidence."

"I like your white sofa. It's fine sitting here, maybe finer
when we are walking together."

"Yes, but not yet."

"Of course not. Just sitting till the time turns right." Dyer said. "And sometimes the time doesn't turn right. I suspect you know that already, a woman of your experience and longevity. Longevity itself doesn't turn right, does it?"

"We're here aren't we Mr. Dyer? So that says something in favor of longevity, doesn't it?"

"Wisely put, Tine, wisely put and worth pondering over the immediate short haul."

"I have no idea what you're saying, but I do like hearing you say it."

"Oh, I've been accused of being a talker, that's true enough. And putting sentences so they interlock and sprint on their own does excite me. It's like the scent of fresh woman in the afternoon sun along a beach, walking not by herself but in the company of an equally elderly fellow with scraggily short legs not at all protected by some scruffy khaki shorts. Occasionally wobbly legs. Did your beloved Harry have those?"

"Leg cramps during sleep."

"They're the worst, insufferable and overwhelming, don't you agree?"

"I've never had them."

"Maybe women don't but I can give you a splendid minute by minute account itself so startlingly alert that you watch the muscles in your leg ripple toward their fruition of bulging, throbbing according to mysterious dictates unknown to you or your various ministers of healing, with their stupid salves or silvered socks etc. etc."

"Why Mr. Dyer, I hadn't realized what a medical expert you were. And how did you become that way?"

"Long study in the best medical schools in Egypt and this country," Dyer said smiling over his cooling tea mug.

"Does that mean you speak Arabic?"

"Like a sheik, like a Saudi prince, don't you know?"

"You're not at all like my Harry. Not at all."

"And for that you're thankful. I can tell. You're profoundly thankful. I bring new dizziness into your staid life, don't I?"

"Perhaps. Perhaps not."

"A barbed reply and entirely worthy. Is it time for our walk?"

"Because you feel defenseless sitting?"

"Yes, assuredly. And more importantly I've noticed on this key that the optimum time for heat is 2:30 to 4 p.m. For the bathing heat that smears out the muscles so that a 3 a.m. they have no inclination to bunch up, cramp, or startle you into pain."

"I've not had such pain. Don't you remember?"

"But I have, and I want to walk it off."

"So it's not company you want, but only the exercise against anticipated pain."

"Your company is my pain cure, my escape from cramping, my deliverance into the soft meadow of straight forward hiking. And look at us, we've made no progress toward just getting up from this wondrous couch."

4.

The Gulf of Mexico was a cookie sheet grey slab, still but occasionally flecked by distant chrome nubbins; the sun was a gold-red disk backlighting the nubbins and searing into their squinting eyes. "It's what God looks like," Dyer said, "put on a veil or you'll be blinded—despite your dark glasses."

"You're no Moses," Tine said quietly.

"So you found me out," Dyer answered. "But we could, if we believed, walk right out on this water and catch the sun in our hands, couldn't we?"

"You go first."

"I'd rather dig for sand fleas."

"You and Harry both. He used them for bait, he did."

"We could pause for fishing if that be your wish. I conjure that you often did so with Harry."

"Never."

"Good. We can skip duplication and find what's truly right for us. I say a tough passage to get by the Kohl estate. What do you think?"

"I never went near the place only looked at its formidable dock."

"Then, let's give it a spin. The boulders of the dock are a challenge. We'll half-swim around them. That's what I'd advise and I speak from significant experience. We'll go down the beach until the fencing on the dock makes passage, what should I say, more challenge than we need in our dotage?"

"Speak for yourself."

"I always do, and clearly."

"You have excessive confidence, Charles Dyer."

"You give it to me, and I feel I can float free with you. Is that the case?"

"I don't know the case you mention."

"Nor do I, subtle woman. Let's just walk and talk and see."

An enormous patch of clouds passed before the sun and the sky turned red orange with torn billows allowing soft bright white light through. They entered only a foot into the sullen Gulf and smiled at their cold toes treading the softest sand, the mildest salt sea.

Dyer said, "The great beast is having a very quiet day, as if to celebrate our pathetic disturbance of his surface."

"Her surface," Tine corrected him.

"Of course, I should have noticed, did naturally notice but misspoke—the sea's always mother."

"Not necessarily—beyond mothering is simple companionability."

"As in, here we are together, facing the Kohl's dock. So now let's submerge into this cool water and semi swim out

and around Kohl's clumsy edifice against beach intruders."
And Dyer shoved off into the silent, still Gulf waters. His slow
winding churn sending gentle ripples against first the big jag-
ged rocks lining the dock and then the posts driven down onto
narrow pilings. He reached the end of the dock and took hold of
a ring mounted at water's edge on the last post. He waved back
at Tine who had come only two thirds of the 200 feet of barrier.
"You can make it," he shouted.

"Is it worth the effort?" she answered slowly, but loudly.

"Of course it is, if we want to get to the south end, to the
overgrown hotel."

"Maybe you're the only overgrown thing near me."

"Of course I am! Growing all around you. Enveloping you.
Dragging you under to show you sights you couldn't have imagined. Ones we might not survive."

"Only if we so choose. Isn't that so?"

"Of course, only if we so choose. And choose we should,"
Dyer said and repeated, "Choose we should. So catch up and I'll
tow you around down the other side."

Finally she extended her right hand already wrinkled
from the soft water, and her white, silken flabby arm which he
grabbed by the forearm. He yanked and took her around the
end of the dock.

## 5.

When Spradlin brought the cash drawer back to Jimmy that
night he remarked that neither Tine nor Charlie had come back
to the store. At first Jimmy simply nodded to the news but after
an impressive pause he said, "I wouldn't worry about it. They're
two grownups wouldn't you say?"

"Yes," Spradlin answered.

"Yes," Jimmy repeated. "We can start worrying tomorrow if
we don't see them. I've been thinking when I was in the war. In

the Philippines—maybe in Cebu, maybe Manila, I can't remember, but on the beach and we had a badly wounded Japanese soldier lying on the sand with his intestines spilling out and some of us were kicking him. He was writhing around trying to cram his guts back into his open side, as if he could reassemble himself and run away. But someone went on kicking and cursing, treating him like some abandoned animal, some partial road kill. It was awful and I could only imagine that maybe on the other side of island Japanese soldiers were doing the same thing to some wounded G.I. And I thought that made it acceptable. I was thinking that all afternoon, looking at my blue vinyl-liner pool and drinking cold medicine. Is that crazy?"

"Yes, that's crazy" Spradlin said.

"Don't ever call me crazy." Jimmy said with fake menace.

"Sorry."

"You're not really sorry, but that's okay. If they're not back, you can send Earl after them before he locks up for the night. You can send Earl after them, and if you do, which I think you ought to, then tell Earl there's a new machete—came in last Saturday, which I put in the meat locker right next to the door on the right. He'll like the heft of it."

"Why a machete?"

"For the jungle undergrowth. I'm pretty sure Dyer will take her to the abandoned Ringling Hotel on the south end. Dyer likes to spend time there. Its loss of grandeur speaks to him—his bliss among ruins."

"Maybe you and Charlie are both crazy."

"I told you not to say that." Jimmy laughed. "You might have to cram your insides back inside and scurry away to the Colony Beach Club."

"I'd rather lie on the sand and writhe and howl."

"With Earl piecing you up for Gulf sharks."

## 6.

When they reached the beach on the south side of Kohl's dock, Tine and Charlie lay on the sand for almost a half hour.

"You can't see it, but it's there," Dyer said. "If you can get the right angle through the tallest cabbage palms you can see what remains of the final top cupola—a cement skeleton 35 abandoned years old. Maybe you can't see it, but you can almost feel it, can you?"

"I'd rather soak in this wondrous sunlight," Tine answered.

"Of course you would, of course you should."

"Good then we don't have to go further, do we?"

"Oh we do. We do. It's our destiny, to spend our last few minutes on this planet wandering among the wasted dreams of a circus master with a far better mustache than mine. But without my chin whiskers."

"Oh, I like your bristles, Charlie Dyer. But let's rest a while in this low, soft sunlight."

"No. On your feet and forward to our destiny. Forward to colonnades amid empty lobbies and abandoned reflecting pools, the expansive home of tropical fish, and endless stairs up to a skeleton cupola with its launching bridge to marble steps 80 feet below. And looking out at St. Armands, as well as Sarasota Bay, and the bridges back to mainland stability. Everything around us just greenery and dreams and ended visions. In 8th grade I used to picnic evenings in the ghost hotel. Kids plunged to their death from rail-less steps or in open elevator shafts and even off the perch overwatching the waters. Youngsters' bodies broken around columns, left for ficus to feast on. And scrub mangroves. In the empty lobby's pool, we can imagine multi-colored mini- fish—not too high an imaginative leap."

"What fantasies you conjure, Charlie Dyer! Stay with me here on this warm sand, this soft sunlight."

"Not a chance. We're heading for the final jetty. The last outpost of this new world, the end barrier to the primeval and the visionary. Unbelievable dreams did old John Ringling have in mind—a universe he could conjure up, populate, embellish, worship and, and," Dyer paused overlong for effect, "And abandon. Toss away like some polluted Kleenex, like some embarrassed expectorant, a sniff, a drool, a fart. Like a fart in a crowded room. And plenty, my lady, wanted to be in that room, too. Plenty were giddy for his offenses."

"Not I."

"Of course not, my lady, my sweet princess of the wrinkles. You'd have known a Ringling fart was not perfume, if you can excuse my vulgarity, can you?"

"Can I indeed? Come, lie down with me on this cool sand and we can decide."

"No! If you want to see the ghost hotel, and I surely think you do, we must be off immediately. When the light fails we follow."

"I'm tired."

"Oh. Okay let's rest a while until fair lady is refreshed." Dyer lay back down.

"You surprise me, Charlie Dyer."

"I surprise myself around you. And that's a very good thing, I think."

"Let's not think."

"Agreed. Thought's a bust, isn't it? An impediment to everything else. An impediment to understanding how fine it is to lie on hot sand with a beautiful lady and watch the sun set."

"You're constant defining the situation gets in the way of your sweet soul, I do believe."

"If you can't set the situation how can you know the deepest feelings you have?"

"I'm tired of being run over."

"Lady you could never be roadkill. Not even Earl would concede you that status."

"You know Earl, apart from your apprenticeship?"

"I intuit his danger, with, lamentably, some prior validation."

"About which I prefer to know nothing."

"There's nothing about me you don't know already, even if you wish to dismiss it."

"Defining me again, Charlie Dyer. Be careful lest you get cast into my unhappiness with Harry. Especially at the end."

"Ah, at the end," Dyer said quietly, "Doubtless where we are and both know and don't know it, do we? The last wrapping up as the majestic crimson clouds swirl beyond our squinting eyes. The stumbling recognition it's all over even as we savor it so sweetly. Maybe that's its sweetness. Its over-ness. Total over-ness. Old Ringling's greatest gift—his clear sense when something was over, when something need to be ended and ended immediately without any further consideration. The hurricane of 1926 hit and instantly he knew he had an irrevocable choice: end the mansion on the main land or the hotel dream on the island. Personal mansion or public hotel. One or the other. Not both. One only. One only," Dyer lingered over the phrase. And then abruptly got up. "So let's go look at the abandoned dream. Maybe sixty days, maybe eighty days from completion. The very tiles in place, the marble stacked in squares beside the cabbage palms that almost miraculously escaped decapitation, since their placement complemented his vision precisely where they were. Offering succor from the stark sunlight. So up you go, my lady. Opulence awaits us; we need only fill in the blanks and cut away the sturdy encroaching mangroves, the thick swamp reeds and an occasional rattle snake and its lithe black stalker."

"Lithe black stalker, whatever do you mean, Charlie Dyer?"

"The big black ones eat rattlers. They're unaffected by venom."

"Like us?" she asked.

"Just like us, Madame. Just like us." He yanked her to her feet and they set off down the sharp shelled beach.

When they had reached the interior of the hotel, Dyer gestured sweepingly across the empty reflecting pond and pointed to the distant pillars marking off the large octagon that would have been the focal point of the lobby. "Ever seen such distances so carefully laid out so that sunlight and sweet breezes could pass through, ruffling the water and infusing the air with a tenderness you might only imagine if you had spent the evening in a Gardenia garden? What must he have seen in his sharp mind's eye standing here and realizing everything would have to stop? Knowing the stairs would remain rail-less, the tiles never unpiled, and the cleared jungle so savagely reconstructed in a sore decade of strangling his ultimately greedy longing. And the tiles stolen by kids and contractors, cops and tourist adventurers. Swell urinations on his colonnades. It's too miserable for recounting, so let's take a look upstairs. You'll like the view, my lady, all the way past the Kohl estate, past the Rus-Mar motel, past Jimmy's Beach Cart—all the way to the trailer park, maybe all the way to Anna Maria, though I doubt it."

"You know the landmarks, don't you, Charlie Dyer? But I'm worried about the open stairs, and they don't look well braced."

"But I am, so just take my arm, and we'll take 'em slow and safely, holding on to each other. If one goes the other will join in, and won't that be a bit exciting and maybe appropriate for two already joined in disconnection."

She asked while taking firmly his left arm, "Disconnected? How?"

"Harry cut you loose, letting you wash away on some jetty somewhere, ash white like driftwood or a shell that shed its innards months ago."

"Too hard on me, Charlie Dyer. Too hard on Harry." Tine paused after the first three steps and just as Dyer was about to chastise her lethargy, she said, "Way too hard on Harry, a very good man, if a bit willful and stupid about things."

"Stupid?"

"Not clear in his own mind what outcome he wanted to follow on his assertions. Not every time, but often enough to be noticeable."

"Noticeable by you" Dyer said taking the next step, "and he didn't acknowledge that did he?"

"Charlie Dyer, I do believe you listen to me better than anyone I know."

"Good. So we can take next steps together. On these stairs and beyond, way beyond." Dyer pointed beyond the cabbage palm tops as they reached the opening of the octagonal gazebo on the roof. "Come step to the edge with me. We like the edge don't we? After all, on the edge is all that's left for us, isn't it?"

"Maybe for you Charlie Dyer, but you don't speak for me."

"Of course I don't. How could I? A runt of man imitating a human being."

It seemed like something akin to compassion flickered on her lightly sweating face, as if for a moment she realized something, everything, had been difficult for Charlie Dyer. With evident surprise she put an arm around his back. "We could go to the edge," she said. "We could do it. It wouldn't be hard, would it? Just a step off."

"My lady, you scare me. You know so much, see so clearly, and know so thoroughly the story is almost done. But before we can get to the edge, stop and listen carefully. Don't you hear it?"

"Hear what?"

"Stop speaking and listen. You'll hear the steady thwacking sound, someone cutting through the ficus, through the mangroves' dried edges getting to the hotel."

"Someone coming to save us? Or someone to join our jumping?" she asked. "I don't think we should wait to see."

"I think we should wait."

"No! Come bundle with me, Charlie Dyer, and we'll skip out onto the jutting platform above the concrete sea and

holding each other so tightly we'll settle slowly into a swoon-
ing splatter. Five storeys down and a delightful impaling. Yes! A
marble mauling. Take hold. Take hold."

"Not a chance," said Dyer, writhing a bit in her surprising encirclement, and resisting her lunge toward the void's lip
platform.

"You can't, won't, resist me. It's what we both know we've
wanted for so very long. Don't fight it. Help us lunge toward it."

"Dyer! Dyer!" Earl shouted; he had emerged from the
chopped thicket and stood staring up in front of the hotel's
desolate entrance.

Immediately Tine released her grip, abandoned her direc-
tion and looked over the platform edge. "It's Earl," she shouted.
"It's Earl, come to save us."

"Save me," Dyer said.

"Oh, you silly man. Extrapolating from nothing. Nothing
at all. Earl! Earl! You come up here now. We'll show you the
most extraordinary view. When you get here, it will change
everything."

When he reached the skeleton gazebo Earl was sweating
and breathing heavily. "Lot of damn cutting," he said quietly,
sitting down on the concrete bench lining the gazebo.

"Nothing's changed," Dyer said.

"Oh, it has! Everything has," Tine said. "Earl's here, and
we're saved."

Earl nodded, "I cut us a path back to Jimmy's truck."

"Of course!" Tine said, "Now we don't have swim, or
worse— walk back. We have a truck—Jimmy's truck. We have
Jimmy's truck. Jimmy thinks of everything."

"Well," Earl said, "I think Jimmy, or somebody, shellacked
the vinyl seats and they're pretty cracked up. Uncomfortable."

7.

"I see the truck's back," Spradlin said when he picked up the cash drawer the next morning.

"Yes," Jimmy said, "I heard them come in later, but I was in bed. I figured Earl would either save them or slaughter them."

"And you didn't care either way."

Jimmy laughed a bit and said, "I always liked Tine and Harry. Earl and Charlie less so."

"You're a hard case, Jimmy Faneuf. And with enough nudging I bet I could get Earl to take you out. He likes to carve things up."

"Earl's in my pocket, just like you, sometimes. So I'm not worried. Just thinking about that Japanese kid trying to put his innards back in place, rinsed in blood and squealing and gagging. Why was it arranged for me to see that? What was I supposed to carry away?"

"Maybe only so you could tell me about it, and seem profound and worried, maybe noble."

"I like seeming noble. It suits me, don't you think?"

"It's better than your yellow bathrobe."

"You might have a cruel, unattractive streak."

"Maybe so, but one thing I do know. Charlie took a shower last night. You should ask him about it."

"I think I'll pass on that. But I'll be in the shop for the lunchtime rush."

# Chapter Two

It was well after the lunch time rush (itself in September an in-house joke) that Charlie Dyer showed up.

Spradlin said, "You seem well-showered. Perhaps you could tell us about it."

"No shower at all. We went swimming, we did, Tine and I."

Jimmy said, "But she hasn't come in for her morning paper . . ."

"Maybe it takes a while for her to recover from a man like me," Dyer said smiling insanely.

"More likely it takes a while to fumigate her place back to normal after an overnight with Charlie Dyer," Spradlin said.

"Haven't heard that phrase 'overnight' since, maybe, 7th grade. 'An overnight' pretty exotic, a favorite word—inexperience talking, don't ya think?"

Turning away, Spradlin said, "You're a poet, Charlie Dyer."

"Some women think so."

"We'll ask Tine, when she comes in. Ought to be fairly soon now."

"I'd never put a schedule on it," Dyer said.

Jimmy said, "I suppose ecstasy has its own time clock."

From his butcher's case Earl called out, "She was cold and wet last night."

"She'll be in soon enough and clarify everything," Jimmy added, ending the conversation.

Spradlin emptied a few hanging pails, and Dyer seemed busy bringing forward paper towels and napkins from a side room beyond the meat locker. Banter filled in the customerless hours till six o'clock.

"So who's going over to check on her?" Jimmy asked.

"That's not called for," Dyer said. "Not called for. She's her own person and surely doesn't have to be looked after."

"I thought you might care," Jimmy said.

"I didn't say I don't care. I didn't say that. I respect her privacy. She has her own life. That's all I was saying, and having said that I think one of us ought, I suppose, to go knocking on her door, just to make sure she's full and fit and ready to face this hostile world."

"I don't see anything hostile in the Beach Cart," Jimmy said.

"Except maybe Earl," Spradlin said.

"Listen, Earl was very helpful to us last night. Very helpful. Very thoughtful."

"So why don't you and Earl go over and see that's she's full and fit and happy to see you." Jimmy more or less commanded.

When they left and were beyond the shell driveway, Jimmy said to Spradlin, "You know damn well they did something to her last night, don't you?"

"Like what?"

"Like something out of your pale imagining."

"You're crazy."

"I told you not to call me that, didn't I?"

"You did."

"Then why are you saying it?"

"Because you're saying crazy things. I think you're still sick."

"How sick is this: from the meat locker get one of the long plastic bags for lamb legs, and take it to my truck and see if the machete is in the truck some place. Maybe under the seat or maybe in the back somewhere. If it's there, put it in the plastic sleeve by picking it up, but only from the point, not the handle. Just the point."

"You're serious?"

"Absolutely—just do it. And be quick before they get back. Because they won't spend much time at Tine's house. She's not there."

"How do you know that?"

"Every morning she comes over to pick up a paper. Been doing that for at least five years—even the whole time Harry was sick and after. Just go and get the machete."

When Spradlin came back with the machete in its clear plastic bag, Jimmy threw him a packet of keys and said, "Put it in my locker and be quick about it. They'll be back soon. Do it now."

Spradlin was used to Jimmy's peculiar sense of urgency. He made a bit of racket closing the locker so that Jimmy'd know the task was done. Then he lingered by the meat locker to compose himself and sort through Jimmy's motivation. On the way back he saw through the front glass doors there was another spectacular Gulf sunset, a lurid red—orange flood of broken clouds blistered from behind by a searing sunshine. The billows flashed chrome white at the top edges rendering Earl and Charlie just stick figures coming back to the store.

"The lady's not at home," Dyer shouted as he came in.

"Nobody home," Earl echoed.

"Of course not," Jimmy said. "Of course not. Why don't you tell me what happened?"

"We dropped her off." Dyer said. "We watched her go in, didn't we, Earl?"

"Yeah," Earl answered. "We watched her go in."

"Tell me about how you watched," Jimmy said.

"We watched from the truck. I reached across her and opened her door for her. "Dyer said.

"Yeah," Earl echoed. "Yeah. We watched her go in."

"And yet she's not in the house now, is that right?"

"Yeah," Earl said.

"The place is empty," Dyer added. "Completely empty."

"Then, where is she?"

"I dunno," Earl said.

"Maybe she went out to St. Armands," Dyer said.

"Is her car in the car port?"

"Yeah," Earl said.

"But she's not there, is that correct?" Jimmy asked.

"Not there," Earl said.

"So where is she?"

Jimmy waited for an answer and when none came, he pressed ahead, "So why don't you tell us what really happened at the ghost hotel. What really went on at the Ritz-Carleton last night."

"There's nothing to tell," Dyer answered. "We drove her home and watched her go in."

"We watched her go in," Earl emphasized.

"That's your story then?"

"Yeah," Earl said.

"That's the truth," Dyer said.

"Earl, bring the truck by when you close up. I'm going home now, unless . . . unless you boys have something else to tell me about Tine. Do you?"

"No, we do not," Charlie Dyer said levelly.

"We don't," Earl said.

When nothing further was said, Jimmy went home.

2.

At 9:30 that night, Jimmy in his yellow robe, invited Spradlin in with the cash drawer and told him to get a white plastic inhaler atop a stack of Southern Living magazines on his bureau in his bedroom. Spradlin knew this was a ruse played each time he brought the cash drawer. Jimmy didn't want him to see where he hid the drawer in the kitchen. Spradlin thought about exposing the game just as heard heavy knocking on the front door.

"Earl, just put the keys in the mailbox. I'm about to go to bed." Jimmy shouted.

But the knocking continued three quick times signaling, Jimmy understood, that Earl was not to be put off. Jimmy got up, re-hitched his robe and went to the door. "I said I was going to bed. Didn't you hear that—" but Jimmy stopped himself in mid question, since Earl was rubbing his eyes and crying. For a moment Jimmy thought Earl would rub the truck's key ring directly into his right eye. "Gimmie the key, for God's sake, Earl, what's got into you?"

"She swam away from us." Earl said softly. "She swam way out."

"You're telling me about Tine?"

"Yes, yes," Earl sobbed. "She swam away from us. Way out. Way, way out and then we couldn't see her. Charlie kept calling her. She didn't answer. She was way out. Way, way out."

"You mean in the channel before St. Armands?"

"Maybe. It was dark. We couldn't see much. Couldn't see her anyway."

"Current there could have taken her out into the Gulf." Jimmy said, trying to imagine her voyage. "And Charlie thought it was better to say you dropped her back at her house?"

"Charlie thought she'd get there."

"On her own through the Gulf, in the dark? Really? By now she could be in Mexico."

Earl continued sobbing. And Jimmy took the keys out of his hand, tossed them to Spradlin, who slowly edged away toward the kitchen.

"Come in for God's sake. I've got to call Chuck."

"Chuck?"

"Stover. Chuck Stover our only police officer. Maybe he can get a patrol boat and divers out into the channel."

"It's too late." Earl sobbed.

"Of course it's too late. Too damn late, but processes have to be followed. You get that, don't you? And stop crying. Helps nothing. Nothing at all."

Earl slumped down on the rattan couch, and for a moment Jimmy worried that the rust colored cushions would be dirtied by Earl's old jeans. Before that fret could take deeper hold Earl sobbed more loudly and said, "We killed her. She never hurt anyone, cared about everyone and we killed her."

"Stop it, Earl. Stop it now. You didn't kill her, the tide got her, the current got her. The damn Gulf got her. You and Charlie had nothing to do with it."

"We had everything to do with it."

"How? Did you put her in a boat and haul her out into the channel? Don't be shy. You blackjacked her first? Sob over there. I'm going to call Chuck Stover. He'll save her. Don't worry, Earl. Everything's going to be all right. Just sit there." Jimmy went into the kitchen and then with exasperation said, "Knock off the moaning, Earl. I can't hear Chuck. Just shut it down, will you? For God's sake just shut it down!"

And Earl throttled back his moaning, as Jimmy explained things to Chuck Stover. And when Jimmy came back into the living room, Earl was bent forward holding his head in his hands and apparently still lurching from slow sobs.

"I told him it all happened tonight. Just now so divers might really make a difference. I think he can get that in motion with the Sarasota cops or maybe state troopers out of Tampa or

Venice. So stop crying, Earl. It's unbecoming for a man of your demeanor."

Earl looked up, "What's demeanor?"

Jimmy sighed, half laughed, "Appearance. Your appearance. You look like a really tough guy and here you are sobbing like a hurt girl scout, as if somebody took your cookies away. Did they?"

"No."

"I knew it. So why don't you tell me what really went on last night? Chuck might buy the swimming story, but I wouldn't. In fact I don't, so why don't you spill the actual beans?"

When Earl didn't reply, merely put his head back down in his hands on his knees, Jimmy continued, "I see. You need Charlie Dyer here to spin the story out. Why don't you try it on your own? I'm betting you can pull it off. Probably you and Charlie rehearsed it enough, to get her way, way out there convincingly. But why not skip over that story and give me the true version? You chop her up, Earl? Did you? Or Did Charlie?"

Spradlin was interested that he himself had imagined Earl as a human butcher.

After a few more seconds, Earl said, "We never chopped her up. Never. Couldn't do that to such a beautiful lady. Beautiful lady and gentle, so gentle. She swam way out."

"To get away from you? Isn't that so? She knew what you and Charlie had in mind, didn't she?"

"No. No. No, she swam out because, because . . . it was so beautiful a night. She said she wanted to see the hotel from the water just as everything darkened."

"That's a line Charlie wanted you to say."

"No, he didn't. It came naturally. She was so gentle."

"Nothing came naturally to you, Earl. You better sharpen your story before Chuck gets here. He'll see right through it. He's a city cop, used to hearing stupid stories. Stupid, made up stories."

"It's not made up."

"Just stupid."

"Not stupid. The truth. It's the truth. She swam far out and then we couldn't see her. Couldn't find her."

"So you searched?"

"Of course."

"How?"

"We swam out. We swam around. We looked around. We dove down a bit."

"Just a bit?

"Enough to know she wasn't there."

"Why'd you cut her up?"

"No. We didn't. She just swam out, way out."

"To get away from you and Charlie?"

"No. Why do you say that? She just swam out to see the hotel from the water. I told you that."

"She swam like Hell to get away from you and Charlie. She was terrified, wasn't she? So she swam like fury, like a cyclone on the water to get as far away from you as possible and when she saw you were coming after her she slipped under water and never came up. Right? And for damn good reason, too and you know it, don't you? You and Charlie know it, don't you?"

"No. Why are you saying that? What's wrong with you?"

"There's nothing wrong with me. Just tell Chuck your story. Maybe he'll believe it. I won't. Never will. Why did you cut her up?"

"We didn't. We didn't. She's out in the Gulf. Way out. We couldn't find her."

"I bet the sharks could, after you cut her up. Used her like chum to summon them."

"No. No. Come on. Why are you saying this?"

"Forget what I'm saying. Just make sure you've got it down pat, what you're gonna tell Chuck. You better have it done pat.

Solid. Rehearsed and solid. He'll see through it, and then what are you gonna do? What?"

## 3.

Chuck Stover's face was extensively pockmarked but none the less sagged beneath his tired eyes listening to Earl's story. Just listened and then later to Jimmy said, "You know in Philly when you had a killing, you'd go and grab somebody and shake 'em till they gave you a lead, but here there's nobody to shake."

"Well, there's Charlie, and maybe a body somewhere." Jimmy said.

"So maybe I'll shake Charlie when he comes in tomorrow."

"You do that and maybe everything or nothing will break open."

"Yeah, nothing. Even the Sarasota cops want to wait another day, figuring it's some kind of lover's quarrel."

Jimmy said, "Tine Peverill, a runaway. I love it. You know Earl's lying."

"Earl's too dumb to lie."

"Charlie's a good instructor. I bet he told Earl to keep shouting, 'way out, way out.'"

"He said it often enough."

"It's their way out. Way, way out."

"In Philly, we had a domestic case in an apartment near Bannister where Carlo—I think it was Carlo, maybe Jose, or maybe Jesus—took a Ginsu saw tooth breadknife to his girl-friend—I assume it was his girlfriend. Damn near decapitated her, then slashed her very pregnant belly to let everything out all on to the green linoleum kitchen floor. Helluva mess. Everything pouring out and blackish and sticky as hell. And thinking about it I realized the Gulf is our friend."

"Yes," Jimmy said, "the Gulf is our friend, our very cleansing friend. So I guess we'll wait another day before the Sarasota cops authorize the expense of divers to search our friend."

"More likely they'll say since a day passed, there's no point sending divers, expensive divers. That's how we thought in Philly."

"Crafty thinking in Philly," Jimmy laughed. "Even craftier thinking on little Longboat Key."

After Stover left, Jimmy felt deflated, drained of any humor. He motioned for Spradlin to sit opposite him on the couch. "I could see you were half laughing at Earl's recitation. But humor is really a stupid device to fend off death. Surgeons I've heard crack jokes as their patients die. Cops make jokes kicking over corpses. Chuckling covers a lot of sins, doesn't it? I could see Tine fending off Earl's hacking—"

"Not exactly a chuckle-fest," Spradlin said.

"I could imagine her limbs floating slowly to the Gulf's floor. I can imagine Charlie planting seeds in Earl's little brain. I could imagine it, but maybe not really."

"Yeah, not really," Spradlin echoed.

"I could imagine she'd try to re-attach her arms, using one hand to recollect the other. Trying to collect innards, shoving them back into her stomach, hoping she had more agile fingers to find all her parts nestled in the cool Gulf. You know about twice a year I swim way out into the Gulf, far enough out that I can't quite decide if I've gone too far, and sun setting in the scarlet sky and I think of him scampering on the Filipino beach while we kicked him—and I think in the Gulf he'd have a chance, the cool Gulf would provide the reattaching glue. Healing waters. Our friend the Gulf. My friend the Gulf and sometimes I'm taken out of the warm water and alone above in a kind of rapture of the sky and I imagine I see him carefully going through miraculous repair and then swimming, stroking with greater energy and enthusiasm toward the horizon of his friend the Gulf. And he turns and shouts to me a thousand feet above him. He shouts, that delicious Asian mispronunciation: 'Sank you! Sank you!' Sank indeed! Jesus, they killed that sweet old lady."

"That's crazy."

"Get out of here. I told you never to say that."

# Chapter Three

O n Thursday mornings Spradlin played tennis at The
Colony Beach Club with two doctors and his old boss,
Lem (short for Lemuel) Jelliffe. The doctors, Burton (Buzz)
Clanton, a dermatologist with a slow, fiercely spinning, arching
southpaw serve, and Irving Nasr, a pediatric surgeon with an
avocation of Sufi mysticism, made a logical tandem for Lem's
lust for acquisition, and Spradlin's confusion about life's pur-
poses. Buzz unfailingly referenced his pillared home on Siesta
Key and his stable of Mercedes and seemed a perfect target for
Lem's continuous real estate grifts; Spradlin a sponge for Nasr's
cryptic references. All four, appropriately enough, were hyper
competitive. Bayfront possible acquisitions floated quickly
among angled service returns and deft net poaches—each one
celebrated with gruff taunting.

Buzz had the strongest game, a rather endlessly steady,
forceful topspin forehands and a perfectly flexible two handed
backhand that he could vary surprisingly between slice or flat
drive in a nicely camouflaged way. It was clear from Buzz's
consistency and ever-increasing torque that he could easily
dominate the other three in any singles test. But in doubles
his evident fierce dominance was nicely complemented by Irving's dreamy lob-making abilities and his bizarre, occasional

crossing movements that bespoke a strategy too deep for ratio-
nal understanding.

Paired against them Spradlin's sole contribution was an
occasional blazing serve and an equally occasional wrist flick
service return down the line, intimidating Irving when Buzz
served. Lem was steady and far more interested in recounting
losing bids on real estate in the Sarasota/Venice area, or lament-
ing the late expiration of his weekly shopper that he had hired
Spradlin to edit as well as sell ads for. Lem imagined the weekly
he titled The PeliKan as a repository of snobbish gossip among
the keys along the Gulf's coast from Tampa down to Naples.
He claimed he had changed the "c" to "K" as a signal to "mid-
Western lunch pails" that Kansas had been remembered. But
distribution never got beyond Longboat, Lido and Siesta Keys.
It was a feature in the June 6th issue on "Dr. Burton (Buzz)
Clanton, Skin Man," that brought the two together, particularly
Spradlin's questioning caption for the photo of Buzz's home on
sixteen-foot-high piers 146 feet back from the Gulf's highest
tide: "And how many Mercedes are parked beneath the house?"
That particularly thrilled the dermatologist.

The PeliKan was an abortive, four-month experiment.
Spradlin remembered the sweating urgency of trying to con-
vince small business owners to take out an ad in the eight-age
shopper. Summer humidity only fleshed out his embarrassment
at the pitch Lem had rehearsed him to make: "Mr. Jelliffe has
come down from Massachusetts because he's convinced the
Keys will become something like a new state within Florida,
and your ad will, as a founding-initiator, qualify for a special
discount rate extended through the next five month period—
no, make that six months. One inexpensive quarter page ad for
six months exposure in this new venture. You'll be in on the
ground floor, the ground floor. You'll get the classified ads before publication. A single issue might allow you to find bargains
to pay for the ad. It's essentially a freebie. . . ." It was like serving

up a soft underhand floater for Buzz's tennis pasting put-away
. . . was it?

"Pretty ambitious," Jimmy Faneuf told Spradlin when he
learned about the editorship. "Must have some backers somewhere, or he's gonna exploit you even more than I do."

"Not possible," Spradlin replied laughing. "But there's
plenty of family money. Lem has cash and gentility in his background. Jelliffes were key in Boston's earliest China trade, and
Jelliffe Motors sold out in 1910 for a half interest in a car company named General Motors."

"Now tell me Lem told you that himself."

"He did."

Jimmy smiled and nodded. Spradlin scrambled to the
backcourt unsuccessfully running down one of Irving's dreamy,
soft lobs. The ball was out of reach.

Spradlin's sudden lurch of sweat summoned up that summer of unsuccessful sales, as skeptical merchants on the three
keys turned him down. It was not long before Lem announced,
"Whatever you sell will be your salary. I'll keep The PeliKan
going for another two months and if you haven't put things on
a sound footing, I'm done."

When Spradlin complained that sales couldn't support
editorial work in a single person's responsibility, Lem replied,
"Of course not. That's why we're moving on to real estate. Can
you believe Gulf frontage is going for two hundred bucks per
front foot here on Longboat? Two hundred bucks a front foot.
It's worth maybe forty thousand dollars a front foot someday.
You buy it, and just wait for developers to start salivating. Salivating. No more hustling slime wad merchants selling beach
trinkets. We're talking real investments here. Fuck The PeliKan.
Besides you're not into sales. Anybody can see that. You don't
really believe in yourself."

"I don't really believe in myself," Spradlin thought watching the yellow ball bounce softly against the green windbreak hung on the court's fencing.

They switched sides and Lem tossed an extra ball to Spradlin. "Time for the super serve," he said smiling. "Time for the scorcher. Intimidation is the name of the game. Pour it on, big fella. Just like New York. Sell these assholes some beachfront. Always be closing!"

"Fuck you," Spradlin replied, then bounced the ball six times before leaning into his strongest serve wide to Buzz's forehand. As always Buzz answered with a hyper topspin crosscourt; scrambling Spradlin sent his lucky low volley return right at Nasr's crossing body. The crisp volley nicked Irving's racket handle and spun into his midsection. Nasr did not wince, only smiled and pointed upwards as the morning blue sky darkened; a large nimbus cloud had suddenly shielded the sun. Spradlin imagined Nasr did not feel any pain from the shot and admired what he assumed was Nasr's Zen-like dismissal of all hurt.

"Sweet!" Buzz shouted, "how many thousands of dollars did you spend to learn that shot?"

"Natural talent," Lem countered. "Buy high, sell low, and work on volume."

At the 5 to 4 crossover they all sat on the narrow long wooden bench beside the empty umpire's tall chair. They passed two water bottles. Nasr took a long swallow from his purple bottle and passed it to Spradlin. "My trench mouth has pretty well cleared up," he said smiling.

"I Listerined this morning," Spradlin answered.

"You know they couldn't pay you enough to sweat like this. It's quite amazing, isn't it? We're here working our asses off for what?" Lem said.

"To humiliate you," Buzz answered.

"Done long ago," Lem answered stretching his legs out in the red dust of the court.

Nasr waited through the silence and then said, "Childhood humiliation so necessary and sad."

"You're necessary and sad too," Lem said. "I'm closing down The PeliKan."

"You know I never see it on Siesta anyway," Buzz said. "The only issue I've held is the one I starred in." He laughed. "But I'm sorry it's going under. Just like you're going under this set."

"It's not a matter of skill—only your condition." Nasr said. "Sluggish and sad."

"I'm thinking about putting together a consortium," Lem said with surprising loudness.

"Jesus!" Buzz commented, "One venture dies and another is born. You gonna hit us up for that one too."

"I don't need you," Lem said. "Even Daddy likes this one. But let's finish the set. It's the surgeon's serve."

"And that's a blessing," Spradlin said to Lem as they made their way to the backcourt.

And, indeed, Nasr's low, arched American twist serve proved a blessing indeed. The serve came in so shallowly, Lem could step in and paste it directly at Buzz who dove, ducked, doubled over in vain attempts to avoid the drives. Spradlin and Lem easily closed out the set. The next set easily followed the pattern, and after the swift 6–2 victory the four sat again on the narrow bench, sunlight unshielded fused their Moody shirts to their skin.

"Tell us more about Jelliffe real estate ventures," Buzz said to a smiling Lem.

"Not much to tell," Lem said. "Cheap Gulf frontage sells itself. It's just a matter of getting leverage on whatever cash is needed."

"My house on Siesta Key has increased maybe three per-cent over the past three years. I don't see any immediate bargain in buying more."

"That's Siesta," Lem said. "not Longboat. Longboat's much bigger, much emptier, and with a huge parcel and ghost hotel at its thickest end—the end closest to Lido and Sarasota. And much cheaper. If we get a hold of the Ringling Hotel piece, maybe this Colony piece and maybe the Kohl Estate, we've got the Gulf side's future in our hands. Even Daddy, always worried about hurricanes, sees that."

"So, Daddy's in?" Buzz asked.

"I think so," Lem answered, "but even if he isn't, we ought to be, don't you think? This is America and real estate is the surest way to wealth, especially in Florida—quick buck beachfront. What could be easier?"

"So, Daddy's not really in?" Buzz persisted. "And the Ringling heirs are hardly pikers, or at least their lawyers aren't. They'll know what holding can win for them eventually."

"But every time the Sarasota Herald Trib runs a story about some high schooler dying in the abandoned hotel, the wait gets that much longer." Spradlin said.

"Or the possible litigation over teenagers' deaths gets more expensive, or barring that, just the expense of increasing the fencing or the guarding of the property makes the investment, what shall we say, 'less attractive.' And there's always the possibility of a hurricane taking everything away . . . everything except the taxes on the land." Lem said. "Besides everything depends on the pendulum swing, doesn't it? If your Siesta holding isn't on fire, maybe the pendulum is swinging our buyers' way. Here comes the pendulum . . . grab hold, legs lock on ride it to the top of a sellers' release."

"An image as compelling as the clouds above," Nasr said, tossing his head back skyward.

"I don't think they're compelling," Lem said. "Only changing puffs of rain-spill."

"Of course, that's all we see—constantly shifting images but beyond them the changeless sun, the purest forms of our ultimate goodness."

"Ah, that's deep," Lem said smiling. "A pediatric neuro surgeon piped directly into God."

"Sarcasm and bitterness can't long sustain themselves." Nasr said.

'But while they're here, let's enjoy them," Lem added. "Besides, if the consortium flies, I can get you acres more than 10% on your investment, which, incidentally I guarantee as the first-year return."

"On what amount and for how long?"

"One year. One tidy year extendable, and with a two-bedroom suite for your friends to use if we get to that phase."

"You get more interesting every time we play," Buzz said. "And what's the opening bid to get in?"

"I'd have to speak to my people."

"Your people," Nasr said. "Your people. Who are your people?"

"Jelliffe retainers in Miami and Boston. Easy to get along with and always with clever ideas concerning getting money to make money. Multiplying money is their destiny."

"And yours," Buzz laughed. "Or at least that's what you'd like us to believe."

"Believe and gather checks each demi-year. Better yet, (he took special delight in emphasizing the demi) just watch net worth escalate. Nothing's better than escalating net worth."

Nasr intoned something in Persian, or so he eventually said it was Persian. And when they all were in the clammy showers of The Colony Beach Club's locker room, Nasr chanted something in, again, Persian—low moaning tones slicing through the hot mist and lingering in Spradlin's mind like a revelation of the sudden majesty of the world.

"Is that a commitment that you're in for 20K?" Lem asked Nasr while they toweled off.

"I'll speak to my banker," Nasr said, then returned to low moaning.

2.

Lem drove Spradlin back to the grocery store, but he couldn't contain his excitement. "You realize what we just witnessed? Do you? I'll tell you, my first successful solicitation—my maiden effort at venture capital. And from a Muslim? Can God beat it? It's like God calculated Zakat and said to sinner Lem—Here, son, is your cut. You've been such a splendid steward of my infinite largess, here, kiddo, is a little bonus for your efforts. Incidentally, your sins are forgiven."

"Your sins are never forgiven, never expiated, never compensated, Lem. Believe me, never accepted by what surely must be a just God."

"Jealousy doesn't become you. Besides I think you sense that when the time and opportunity come, I'll cut you in on the action, even though your portion, can only be minimal, indeed symbolic, you simpleton lunch pail."

"It was my tennis connections that got you in the door."

"True enough. That's why I'll cut you in sometime."

"As compensation for my editor's entirely absent salary?"

"I'm not talking income here. Get with the program. We can be truly rich."

"You already are."

"But that's a given. I'm talking about achievement here. Swelling net worth here. Leveraging into a new league—the Barons of Longboat Key." Lem pulled into the store's shell drive.

"And I have to stock shelves, and if I'm very good, I'll deserve to man the cash register."

"Don't tell Jimmy yet when you plan to buy him out."

"Listen to the very unkind wind." Spradlin said, exiting the Desoto Lem said he had bought for $325.00 and the dealer's solemn, smiling warranty: "It'll get off the lot."

Jimmy met him at the door. His face was flushed and strangely he seemed to be mouth breathing.

"You feeling bad?" Spradlin said.

"I could have used some help this morning."

"It's my tennis day."

"Oh yes, I should have remembered. The prince's sports morning. Essential to keep him svelte and tanned." Jimmy began coughing.

"How about I get you some water?"

"Yes. Thanks."

Jimmy took the cup and went outside to sit in one of the for-sale plastic chairs along the narrow curb walk of his store. "September's the best month, isn't it? For sitting and smelling the Gulf and leaving the store to its empty self. People say Longboat's booming. They ought to spend September here."

Spradlin stood beside the chair. The tennis left him relaxed, open to Jimmy's observations and somewhat worried about his health.

"What's Lem's scheme this morning? Or are you just going to sell me an ad in The PeliKan?"

"Real estate," Spradlin answered. "Getting a hold of Gulf frontage from the old Hotel through the Colony Beach Club, the Kohl Estate, Tine's house . . . maybe right up to the trailer park. He figures it will be worth a fortune someday."

"He's right. Too bad he's such a fuck-up. He's right about The PeliKan. But he'll never make it work. Too unfocused, too screwed up mentally. Too arrogant. Too spoiled. Too antagonistic."

"You sound pretty judgmental this noon."

"You think so? I'm just getting warmed up. He's a losing connection for you. Nothing admirable there. Maybe some money but nothing admirable."

"What's admirable?"

"Sticking with an idea. Rolling with the waves against you. Building tenacity each day, each moment. Believing in what you're doing. Plodding effort. You have some of that, but you ought to get out of here, off Longboat. Out of this state. This state conspires against all that."

"So why did you come here?"

"I got very tired of Iowa."

"Maybe Lem got tired of Massachusetts."

"Yeah, maybe, but he didn't get tired in a good way."

"Ah, the Jimmy Faneuf good way. Tenacity in the sub-tropics."

"You can satirize all you like but come with me to the back of the store, outback around the side. Just walk with me. A fella took me around there this morning. Actually asked me, very politely to walk back there with him. Like we're doing now. Very politely."

There was a cement shelf behind the building, about seven feet wide holding stacked empty milk crates with a yellow tarp over them. Jimmy leaned against them and pointed to the thick underbrush extending beyond the building. "I think there's mangrove beyond those bushes. I've never walked out there. So, this very polite fellow asked me how far my property extended into the brush. I said I wasn't sure, but I had some drawings I thought somewhere at home. When I bought the land and the store, I'm sure I got some. I paid about eight grand for the whole piece, including the store. He really laughed at that and gave me his card. Arvida. Ever heard of them? I had a feeling I should have said I paid a lot more for my holdings. He seemed serious, polite and serious. Just what Lem can never be."

"I've never heard of 'em. But Lem did get Buzz and Nasr interested in his consortium, sort of. At least they listened to them. After The PeliKan fiasco that was no small feat."

"It's hard to take Lem seriously." Jimmy said. "I've got to put some chairs out here. You know I think it's all mangrove out there, all the way to the bay, but I'm not sure. I don't think anybody has looked at the area except from the water. Maybe I own it all. I bet Eunice demanded maps. She liked maps. Yeah, she would have had the place surveyed. She surely would have."

It was the first time Spradlin had hear Jimmy mention his absent wife's name, and in response to that experience he deliberately did not look at Jimmy, merely stared at his sneakers and waited to see what else Jimmy might reveal.

"Maybe there's not even solid land out there," Jimmy continued. "Just mangroves and water. Why don't you research that? What's this key made of, really? Maybe only what Lem can dream into it. Maybe he's the right fellow for this place. All plans and simple greed. The Florida formula: 'All plans and simple greed.'"

"Lem has plans, no doubt about that."

"Eunice would have seen through him a minute," Jimmy said as if Spradlin was not standing beside him.

Spradlin waited.

At length Jimmy said, "I wonder if pilings work through mangroves."

Spradlin thought: Goodbye Eunice, but said, "Are you thinking of extending the store?"

"I'm thinking a little death might focus Lem. He doesn't know the first thing about what's important, what matters."

"I think he'd argue the point."

"Meaning you'd argue the point. She'd know how to answer you both, but she won't get a chance, will she?"

"I guess not."

"Absolutely not, so let's get back to the shop and figure out how to fill our empty September."

# Chapter Four

Spradlin remembered that Jimmy Faneuf never liked Reverend Bainer Ward's way of talking too loudly. In plaid trousers and black shirt accenting a stained white stiff circular collar, Ward stood before Earl's glass counter and addressed them both as they came in through the back door. It seemed Ward believed he had a voice made for broadcasting. And Spradlin appreciated the gravelly dulcet tone Ward spun out as if commanding privacy beyond the self-conscious resonance.

"I told 'em no tent would be necessary. That was just an expense they wanted to invoke to kill the whole operation. That kind of prevarication I abjure heartily, don't ya know that? That kind of namby-pamby walking around the event. Why not come right out and say it: 'we don't really cotton to revivals; that kind of showboating doesn't belong on Longboat Key. I hear it in your reception, too, Jimmy, despite your pretense of open-ness, despite the sweet way you run this little operation. Come to think of it. You need to think more strategically. How many more customers would my revival bring in, especially in this off season? How many? Let's face it. I'm not seeing walk-in traffic. Are you? We could play baseball on Gulf of Mexico Drive. Nine full innings, couldn't we? Nobody'd come to interrupt, would they? You play ball, son?'" Ward nodded toward Spradlin.

"No, Reverend," Spradlin answered with exaggerated reverence

"Are Christians big spenders?" Jimmy said off handedly, pretending to adjust his cash register.

"When you have naught, even one is welcome. Even one is just one more. That's a fact. That's a fact."

Jimmy said with resignation, "What do you need, Bainer?"

"Paper plates and napkins, two hundred of them."

"As a donation?"

"Of course. The Lord provides the fried chicken and Jimmy provides the plates and napkins."

"And in return, you disappear, right?"

"You won't see me till Easter. That's a fact."

"For the next revival?"

"Of course. When he rises. In fact, God has told me this fallow season for Jimmy will end shortly. Shortly. God's munificence will blaze forth upon this grocery business, not necessarily in that particular line. God knows the profit margins are minimal in that line. But in connection to that business God will show his faithful shepherd the truly unimaginable abundance of the Lord out of the land itself. Yes, the Lord himself will scan the bleak horizon and find that one just soul to reward for his faithfulness; reward beyond all reckoning, beyond all counting, beyond all complex measurement. Literally stupendous prosperity, filled with sweetness and honey, and softest water flowing sweetly too, endlessly into pools of wellness and achievement."

"The earth is the Lord's and his agent is Arvida." Jimmy said, leaving his register and walking directly at Ward.

"Arvida is Baal!" Bainer shouted. "No righteousness there. Only sin! We must join to thwart that monstrosity. We must."

Jimmy laughed and playfully pushed Ward against Earl's display case. "Why don't you save the rhetorical heavy lifting for your blessed revival. You'll get enough loot to get through the winter and Easter will come and the collection then will carry you through to Maine out of the hot weather for a return next fall. More napkins and paper plates. So it goes. We don't have to hear the rationale, do we, John."

"His passion moves me, Jimmy. I want uplifting." Spradlin said. "Wax on, Reverend."

"Jimmy you and your sarcastic sidekick will be upbraided someday, some special Lord's day. His wrath is targeted and appalling."

"So put in a good word for me, Bainer. Some special dispensation, will you? And John get the plates and napkins out of the locker outside."

When Spradlin returned with a garbage bag filled with the plates and napkins, Bainer and Jimmy were still at it.

"You know, Jimmy, you ought to spend more time at Gulf-side Park. They're your real bread and butter during the slow times. They talk about your rotisserie chickens getting them through the fall. They get their staples from you, despite your price gouging. They don't begrudge you that. They understand we have to prop each other up. In Acts the early chapters it's all spelled out—how much we have in common and must have in common just to get through the days. It's only through love and sharing that we all succeed."

"Succeed enough to spend the hottest months in Maine? The coldest months on Longboat?"

"You don't spoil the message, Jimmy. You just drag out your polluted, skeptical soul and lay it out on Gulf of Mexico Drive to sizzle till it's joyously squashed."

"Like a heretical slug splayed out on a flagment in sunny Maine in August." Spradlin said smiling.

"Oh, wallow on in your secular smugness. Your orange flavored doubt. But the mighty Lord will smite you down in your arrogance in your celebrated ignorance. Spend more time with your real people in the park, Jimmy. They're tonic for your confusion and balance, sonny, for your nasty stupid tongue."

"Leave John out of this, Bainer. You're the perfect antidote to my occasionally missing your mini sermons. They're not boring. Not accurate or wholesome either. But sometimes I do miss them, and then you reappear like a sick swallow and remind me what a clown you are. A clown, a mountebank, a sleazeball, squeezing the very life out of marginal folks. I have justification for my price increases, what are yours? A pipeline to God? I doubt it. A pipeline to increasing cash flow. You bet."

"I always enjoy our conversations," Bainer said, taking up Spradlin's offered bag. "And the Lord, the final arbitrar of our days thanks you for your ever-consistent offering to the modest revival. Of course, as always, you're invited, and especially you, my boy, since you need uplift in the most dire need I've ever witnessed. And I've been six decades in the ministry." And he exited dangling the white garbage bag like a reluctant child by his side.

Spradlin walked behind Earl's counter, slid open its right door and picked out a slice of German bologna. As he chewed, delighting in the sour slimy taste, he asked, "How many folks are in the park?"

"Two hundred thirty-nine. Sixty-one families, thirty-eight doublewides, and the rest aluminum singles." Jimmy said.

"You've done market research?"

"The guy from Arvida told me that this morning. Seems they know the lay of the land."

"And how many are born-again?"

"Probably Arvida doesn't know or care about that."

"So how about we take the Arvida guy to the opening of the revival. What's his name?"

"Miles something or other. I don't know how to reach him."

"But you have his card."

2.

That afternoon Spradlin and Dyer watched as two women came out of Tine Peverill's house and started across Gulf of Mexico Drive toward the store.

"That's Birch Peverill. I brought her here." Dyer said.

"In your private jet?" Spradlin asked.

"No. Through my telephone wire. I talked to her. I told her about Harry's death. She's his sister, come to claim the estate.,"

"And the woman with her?"

"A good friend," and Dyer emphasized the *good*. "Marlene something, I didn't catch it first time, still haven't. Long time good friend, if you see what I'm talking about. Very close, very good friend. Maybe life partner or something, you know. That's what Birch says."

"Birch, isn't that a kind of funny, odd name?"

"She says her daddy wanted a boy, so she was named for a tree, and yes, she knows you can substitute a 't' for the 'r' and get Daddy's message to the world."

"Is she one?"

"Not her. No indeed. She's sweet, but Marlene's one, if you catch my drift."

"And they're living in the house?"

"Why not? She got it free and clear. Lem's trying to con-vince them to sell it to him, or lease it to him, or whatever.."

"I think he wants to turn it into some kind of bond."

"I told 'em to stay away from Lem. Jimmy told 'em that too. But they're a headstrong pair. You might notice."

"Unlike you, Charlie Dyer."

"Birch has Peverill flighty loveliness. You probably never saw that. She's a sweetheart. Marlene's a fucking terror. Probably protects her, and maybe she needs protection."

"Certainly, from Lem."

"And Earl. Jimmy says Earl had eyes for Tine. I wonder if that carries over to Birch. Maybe he's mad for Peverills. Nice people, but Jimmy thought Harry was a little slow. But I didn't know him, did you?"

"Only in the store. He seemed pleasant enough. Not a lot of energy. Maybe because he was pretty sick."

"I'm thinking Jimmy's sicker than he lets on," Dyer said. "And I'm gonna ask Birch about it."

As the women came through the glass doors Marlene shouted at Dyer, "You want a cat?"

"You don't mean that lovely snow-white fluffy, do you?"

Birch said, "She does indeed. She's not a cat fancier."

"But that one is so lovable and affectionate. She got right into my lap."

"So that's real attachment. You've got her."

"He does not," Birch said. "So, give it up, Marl. Kitty stays with the house."

Marlene turned up an aisle but said, over her shoulder. "Stranger things have happened. Sometimes when they get old, they just keel over. No reason, just cat fate. Unhappy karma, maybe. Or anti-intervention by distant god." She went on but out of earshot. Birch produced a list and showed it to first Charlie then Spradlin. Dyer got one of the small carts out from its stack at the edge of the store. He wheeled it beside Birch.

"Marl's out of sorts lately. She doesn't like Florida. Maybe the humidity. Maybe the cat. Do you know its name? Tine told me several times, but I didn't retain it for some reason."

"I can think of a reason." Dyer said.

"You sound like Tine. But that's too late now, isn't it? Tine didn't cotton to Marlene. Some kind of bad chemistry. Do you believe that?"

"I do indeed. Karma, chemistry, fellow feeling, empathy—it's all intuition and stronger than we think. Right?"

"Tine said you knew everything, understood everything."

"Really?"

"Yes, of course. She called me right after she met you here. That's why I wanted to come here. Marl wanted to unload the house sight unseen. But I needed to be in a place where Tine had found such . . . such good feeling, I guess, or maybe settled feeling, as if she'd finally found a home. And a big part of that was Jimmy and this store. So, I had to find out. Marl would sell the house right now, tonight, this afternoon, if she could find a buyer. But I'm not going to do it and I'm the executor on the estate. Besides, your Lemuel says he can help me retain title and get income. He's got some way."

"He's not my friend. Don't be saying about that. He's John's tennis buddy. I'm on Jimmy's side about Lem Jelliffe—"

"I know what you're going to say. What Jimmy has already said and said again. But I'm not a fool, and I've got a good hold on what I own on this key. So don't counsel me now. Not at this point."

"Jimmy said you had a good head on your shoulders." Dyer said. "And Peverill sweetness."

From the next aisle Marlene spoke with surprising urgency, "Good God, are we getting into another 'sweet Tine memory moment?' Jesus, I hope not. If it's not the damn cat, it's the so sweet Tine. It's getting old. She's gone. Gone. Isn't that so, Birch? You damn well know that's so. I can tell you. Your fucked-up therapist can tell you. Probably Mr. Charlie Dyer can tell you. So, why not accept it?"

"Marl, please. Mr. Dyer's only trying to help—"

"Okay! Okay! I'll let him. There's a full cart over here, Mr. special Charlie Dyer. Please when the Queen's done shopping, please bring it over to the house. I'm done. Entirely done. I'll see you back at the house, honey. Take care." And she exited through the front doors.

Spradlin smiled and shook his head. Dyer fetched the cart and wheeled to the registrar.

3.

For the next two days, amid turning chickens on the rotisserie Spradlin kept badgering Jimmy for the Arvida card. And once he got it, he took the afternoon off and drove back down to St. Armands to find Armand's Realty on the circle. Miles turned out to be a tall gawky fellow in, apparently, his early 30's but with a slight nervous tick of speaking out of the side of his mouth. In a notch above whisper tone he was in earnest conversation with (startling Spradlin) Lem Jelliffe. "We see the same possibilities, so you're definitely on the right track, but what are your actual resources? Is that too rude to ask?"

"I'm putting together a consortium. Lots of money in the keys. Lots and lots of it."

"I thought it was all going to the new college." Miles smiled.

"Some of it might be. The older money" and on the phrase, Spradlin moved closer, signaling his desire to enter the colloquy.

Lem turned to him, "Meet my tennis buddy, John Spradlin. We play weekly with some medical people at The Colony. You play tennis? " Lem asked Miles.

"Yes," the realtor answered, evaluating Spradlin's clothing and reaching, Spradlin thought, a dismissive conclusion.

"Doctors off of Siesta, there's a gaggle of them out there, and all pretty competitive tennis players. Why not join us some Thursday morning?"

"Your consortium?" Miles asked.

"A part of it. Deborah Kohl is an old friend of my family in Massachusetts."

At the name both Miles and Spradlin smiled and leaned in.

Lem continued, "The largest landowner on Longboat, and she's tight with Ringling people; I've heard that. Is Arvida talking with her?"

"Arvida is talking with everybody, especially folks with Longboat connections."

"It'll be a struggle," Lem said. "The Siesta vision versus something else."

"Oh, I think that fight's long over." Miles said.

"People want Arvida to think that," Lem said. "People like John's boss, Jimmy F."

"You work for Jimmy Faneuf?" Miles asked.

"Yes, mostly at night." Spradlin answered.

"Sittin' on a gold mine," Lem said, with a very mild laugh.

"Mr. Faneuf's an interesting man. I enjoyed talking with him." Miles said.

"I like working for him."

"Jimmy values John enormously." Lem said. "Likes his judgment, listens to his perceptions. He's considerably more than what he looks like."

"Bless you, Lem," Spradlin said.

"I was talking about Jimmy," Lem said.

Miles laughed. "Gentlemen I've got to get back to my clients, so we'll have to postpone things to some future Thursday. I'm assuming you're all of intermediate level, whatever that might mean on the tennis courts at The Colony."

"I'll be delighted by your presence just so long as you don't approach my clients." Lem added.

"Your clients?" Spradlin said to Lem as they walked out together into St. Armands' soft sunshine and neatly trimmed cabbage palms.

"I have my followers."

"Yeah, people trying to get their invoices paid."

"A few of those I concede. But others who figured they're backing a winner."

"What were you seeing him about?" Spradlin asked.

"We were pumping each other. It's me against Arvida. He wants to know what I've got. And I want to know how far along Arvida is in acquisitions. They smell what I smell."

"The soft scent of upper-class Bay Rum after shave?"

"Not particularly funny. But funny enough. I don't think Deborah- Kohl is upper class. Daddy would agree. Neither is too-tall Miles. I bet he was a KA at Gainesville, the kind who stencil 'Go Gators' on their bellies, and who think of pre-adolescent girls as 'eating pussy.'"

"Pretty crude."

"Miles would know what I'm talking about. Shall we go back in and ask him?"

"I have to get back to work."

"You working days and nights now?"

"Jimmy's been sick."

"You'd be sick too, if suddenly your little dream of honest labor on the good earth turned into a blizzard of cash, more cash than imaginable. More freeing cash. More cash than comprehendible so that for the first time you'd be suddenly freed of all care. Enough to make you sick as, as. . . ." Lem strained to find the analogy.

"It would be like walking to the back of the Laundromat and finding God passed out on top of the dryers." Spradlin said.

But Lem shook his head and countered with: "Come with me Tuesday night, a Russian Orthodox Church Social." Lem paused to watch Spradlin absorb his surprise. "The newest part of my consortium . . . maybe. Do you think I can pass as a super patriot? A supreme anti-Communist, mother-loving new American?"

"Not a chance. Jelliffes came over on the Mayflower. You said so yourself."

"Maybe that's why they told me to come ahead. It ought to be a gas and you should be at my side. My chief of staff. Just like old time, eh, Farrar! We could sell them together. On a good night you were a better pitchman than me. Russian exiles have cash in their mattresses. I read that some place. We can sell them fabulous returns. The return of the Romanovs, wrapped in the American flag. And opening their American checkbooks to underwrite the sweet salvation of Longboat Key."

They walked out of the circle, toward the beach, past stained, sandy benches. The mammoth afternoon sent bright flat beams of light directly at them off the mirror-quiet Gulf.

"I can't get enough of it," Lem said.

"Mother Nature, or Dreams of Acquisition?" Spradlin offered.

"Just the sunlight. It wilts your fucking sarcasm." And with that Lem kicked off his sandals, unbuttoned his oxford, blue button-down shirt, undid his belt, dropped his khaki pants revealing black and grey boxer shorts. He sprinted directly into the water. Spradlin with his foot nudged the clothes into a discreet pile and eyed the turned heads of perhaps seventy bodies sprawled on towels around Lem's sprint to the sea. He thought about turning away, avoiding all embarrassment but instead just followed slowly Lem's path to the languid, pathetic lapping of non-waves on the searing white-to-cool-brown shore.

"I'd say come on in," Lem said kneeling in four feet of the Gulf, "but stripping down should be done behind them" he nodded to the sleepy audience, "never in front of them. That's an affront, a kind of in your face action likely to get you arrested."

"I have no intention, but I did want to know if your consortium is going to be centered around the environment—saving Longboat from development, preserving nature for the public?"

"That's how I'll sell it in the trailer parks. To your people. For the rest of us, it will be return on investment. Wealth unbounded. Opportunity to get shut of all care. What all Americans want."

"Even Russians?"

"Absolutely all Russians. As you'll see Tuesday night."

# Chapter Five

"With luck you'll get to hear about it from VanShuten himself," Lem explained to Spradlin as they drove past the long gates of Bird Key in Sarasota Bay. "He says he's going to build a vast concert hall out in the bay so he can watch it from his patio and docks. He claims he's found a new process that stains concrete a brilliant lavender purple tone that infuses the sand interiorly creating a wondrous sparkling effect, and that will set the whole bay iridescent every sunset. He claims it will be more of a tourist attraction than the phosphorescence in the waters around Puerto Rico."

"Sounds like you," Spradlin said.

"I'm hoping to speak the same language. I need his backing. And if listening to hayseeds spouting anti-Communism is what it takes, I'm there already. He has, as they say down here, 'all kind of money.' And better yet, he's got access to even more funds. Hyper patriotism, buddy boy, sits on mounds of cash. Mounds of cash. Buckets of rubles, acres of scheckels. All of it waiting for 'return on investment'. Love of the flag apparently is the key. I bet you didn't know that, couldn't imagine that. Fold yourself in the flag and when you're unfurled—Bingo, there's dollars littering the landscape, right up to the edge of the Gulf.

And who's sitting with toes in the warm red-tide waters but Russians, yes, Ex-Pat Russians."

"Russians?"

"You bet. There's a colony of them from here to Tampa. Second generation winners off aircraft technology. Sikorski got his start down here. You know how? How he got funds to build his wooden helicopter? From the Russian Orthodox Church Community. He sold bonds on a company that existed only his mind."

"Your mentor!"

"I'm not selling machinery. I'm selling land speculation and whopping ROI's. If we win, The PeliKan becomes an in-house organ for the Longboat Real Estate Trust. You get to edit a big slick, sans advertising with a steady client base of sub-scribers limited to three or four hundred. Don't say that doesn't appeal to you. Just don't say it. Just think it a bit. Turn it over a bit in your little mind."

"Fuck you."

"No, no. Fuck them! Wrap the hayseeds in a hyper-flag—out patriot them and bring in the ultra-loyal funding; for the Russians show them how Constitution worship leads to restoring the Tsar; for the doctors explain how Longboat land yields 16-foot stilted mansions on Siesta and Casey Key far beyond the sweaty grasp of local swine. For everybody instant riches or at least the gleam thereof. The gleam thereof . . . a reason to live. You get it, don't you Spradlin?"

"I get it. But it takes more energy than I have."

"I have enough for both of us. So, let's go in there and sell. Sell like the fucking wind and remember Ike's a fellow traveler; Commies control the State Department; The UN is out to blue-helmet the planet; and worst of all the New Math paves the way for rejection of God and all morality. The Soviets are Satanic, so Let Freedom Ring, via phone message for less than a dollar per month. Let Freedom Ring!"

VanShuten's living room was pavilion sized, opening on to an immense screened patio, then deck overlooking a large, kidney shaped swimming pool. In the living room leather-padded folding chairs had been lined up. Spradlin estimated there were a hundred or so. At the right toward the patio was a wet bar and attending bartender, a fellow in a starched white, long sleeved shirt and string tie. At the very front a fellow in yellow trousers and a lime green sweater was speaking loudly into his standing microphone: "We are only now paying attention to the 'instruction' our students are getting. Local PTA's are viper nests. Do you hear me? Viper nests! And the UN! —scum of the earth. A snake in the very heart of Manhattan, spewing its toxins everywhere. And the blessed Warren court mirroring everything that comes slouching out of Moscow, And Ike, well-meaning Eisenhower, but so colossally naïve, out of touch, beholden to handlers behind the Iron Curtain. And Justice Hugo Black. . . ."

But Spradlin had turned away searching for some familiar face. He spotted Buzz Clanton at the bar and about ten feet away Dr. Irving Nasr, looking up at the strange oval mirrors mounted in the rather low ceiling.

Spradlin churned his way through several eddies of guests and came to Nasr. "Can I get you a drink?" Then with calculation and conscious summoning Spradlin recited in English: "I am not the only one who's drunk, what's more/ This wine has intoxicated many others before!"

"Muslims don't drink," Nasr said quickly. "Rumi had something else in mind."

"Even Muslims named Irving?" Spradlin countered, "I could get you a coke or some tonic water."

"Rumi never would have offered. And as for Irving, my father was given to irony."

As Spradlin got a red wine, the speaker expanded his attack on Parent Teacher Associations: "Listen to them as they scissor up our kids' heads, spreading lies about us—shouting to the world we're weirdoes, or trash-talking fools. PTAs advocate abortion, fluoride treatments, even prettying up the name of our favorite Mullet, as if feminizing it would make it tastier. And the garbage quasi socialist curriculum they sponsor."

When he returned to Nasr, Spradlin asked, "What is talking about? Feminizing mullet. What is that?"

Nasr smiled, "State fishing board has renamed mullet fish as Lisa. Apparently its softer, more desirable, a sure-seller among the fish set. It hasn't been met with enthusiasm. Fried Lisa filet is somehow more enticing than fried mullet filet."

The speaker gained volume as the socializing became more intense, "Be sure to listen to this week's message and please tell your neighbors, your friends, your fellow workers about our work—our weekly broadcast via telephone. We've got keep the call-ins increasing. We simply have to keep generating better numbers. People need to know how many double-agents, how many traitors have pervaded our government, even on the local level. A lethal, pernicious ideology is flowing through this nation. A vision of ever larger government bureaucracies dedicated to leveling wealth, and deteriorating our celebrated, private health care to the lowest common denominator. Ultimately an ideology that wants unity with United Nations and the death of private property. An ideology that dictates what we put in our children's mouths, what history our students learn, what mystical reverence is instilled in the notions of world government.

"Only one force here in West Florida is solidly committed to the truth, a truth that will overwhelm the Communist rag, St. Petersburg Times, and the neo-fascist Tampa Tribune. One Force, one magnificent confronter of liberal lies, our own 'Let Freedom Ring.' We reach at least 1,000 per week and a second line will go in shortly, but we need your help to continue our amazing expansion. We've linked up with John Birch Societies nation-wide, especially a very vibrant and energetic one in Clearwater that is holding an anti-fluoride sit-in next

Sunday. We can get a bus for any Ringers who want to join that confrontation.

"But right here in this county we have a malignancy burgeoning before our very eyes, and often (horrifyingly enough) with our own donations. I am talking about the vaunted New College proposed near the Ringling Estate. Yes, a liberal arts repository spewing out its message of sickening tolerance and acceptance of equality and blind subservience to an all-powerful state. Yes, you'd be shocked my fellow Ringers at what your friends and neighbors are supporting. Under the ruse of 'learning' they're pouring out their fortunes to a pipe-dream of astonishing naivety. Or maybe it's not naivety, maybe it's something cleverer, more insidious, more menacing—a carefully indoctrinated belief system of lies and deception and extraordinary range, swarming through our education system, polluting our science, warping our religious beliefs. We need new committed soldiers in this battle for the future of our beloved Republic. And the leaders here in southwest Florida have answered that call. Have they ever! Our phone line of truth is overwhelmed with users, so we'll move quickly to put in a second and a third line, maybe fourth and fifth, as converts move to help us. But more than phone messages we need stalwart investigators holding local politicians and school boards, holding their feet to the fire. We need a cadre of clear-thinkers, steeped in the patriotism of our founding fathers, willing to risk everything to maintain the integrity of our constitution, our sacred documents. Will you join us in that great endeavor? The greatest endeavor since our founding. The martyrs of our creation those who died at Trenton, or Lexington, or Concord, or at sea, cry out for our support, our own willingness to put everything on the line, to suffer the final sacrifice for a just and sacred cause."

Lem whispered, "I'm against final sacrifice, just for the record. I'm a halfway patriot. Let the hayseeds die. But I'm putting a flag on our bonds, if we generate any."

"I don't see these patriots jumping on your real estate bandwagon."

"Maybe we should look into Arvida as a Commie front."

"They strike me as more Amway, than Com-symps." Spradlin said.

"I'm letting Buzz and Irv work the room for me." Lem answered.

"Not reliable, not really committed."

Lem seemed reflective at the remark, "Maybe not. You're probably right. They're not my most promising lieutenants. Dentists are more open to zealotry."

"And dental assistants.

"You're a closet snob." Lem said. "But Buzz opened Naples for us. And Irv knows where the loose capital lies on the west coast, the other west coast, right here. But mostly I need an entrée to VanShuten."

"Jimmy knows him."

"Are you for real? Why? How?"

"I'm not sure. Maybe Jimmy worked for him before he bought the store."

"Are you sure? Does he know about Jimmy now?"

"Probably not."

"So I can tell him. It's my card in . . ."

"If you want to exploit another's illness for your own selfish ends."

"What better cause? Commiserate with the sickly and as a result get a real estate windfall. What could be sweeter? What could be more ennobling? What could be more life affirming?"

"Jimmy's probably only got the flu." And Spradlin turned away toward a new speaker up front, a strikingly young blond woman wearing an orange tank top and clearly hand-sheared jean cutoffs that tracked the inset of her wonderfully tan and sleek thighs.

"Hi Everyone, I'm Valery from Sarasota High's Sailor Circus, and thank God there are no trapezes rigged here. I'm here to let you know how much the Sailor Circus appreciates your support year after year, and to let you know that I'm making a film with some really talented kids from the New College. It's a kind of romantic comedy set mostly on prom night at a famous place on Longboat Key, the old Ringling Hotel, the Ritz-Carleton. We've been making the film forever—nights, weekends, during the summer despite the mosquitoes and I think we're saying something pretty important about the old hotel, about tourism and the future of the west coast of Florida. Soon we're going to have a free showing at the ruins of the hotel itself, since, kind of, the hotel is actually the star of the show. I play a Russian refugee who's come to Florida to avoid being killed by Communist thugs. I turn out to be the love interest of a young director at a college film school, Steve, who couldn't be with us tonight. But he sends his thanks and his very best for all the Russian emigres who make a substantial part of the Let Freedom Ring Movement. Steve can do some of your voice-overs for the phone message, if you want. He's got a terrific resonant voice. And he absolutely believes in what you are doing."

"I know what I'm doing—looking at Valery. We've got to get connected with that film crew." Lem said.

"And what are you doing? Need a tissue, better yet, a towel, a whole Turkish towel?" Spradlin said.

"Jesus H. Christ connections to the film crew and to sacred Valery." Suddenly Lem pushed forward breaking up the Russian conversation of three bearded elderly fellows and without apologizing Lem shouted to Valery: "Does the film say anything about the Commie threat to our way of life? Does it say anything about that? Does it uphold American values, our way of life, or do the Commie thugs win?"

Valery laughed and bellowed back, "Of course it does. The film is an expression of American freedom, American liberty and individualism. It's a hymn to self-righteousness, and the power of the individual to save what's pure and good about our time here on this beautiful beachy planet."

*Beachy planet,* Spradlin thought. To be on that planet with guide Valery pulling bits of sparkling sand from my loins and watching overhead her double spinning on a trapeze. Back and forth with each parabola's apex shedding articles of clothing until, naked and knees lapping the swinging bar, she reached toward him, smiling and laughing and offering a perch above or below her. Yet swiveling beside him on a vast and warm beach towel spread out so that its orange luminosity stretched to the end of the horizon. Spradlin leaned forward, watching Lem push aside others as he lurched toward her.

"Look I've got a consortium of investors who want to back your film and its American message, people who are hungry for your . . . your . . . your romantic comedy, and for the lure of an absolute resort embodied in the old Ringling Hotel. I've got a group of really committed investors—some here want to join already. Investors willing to sacrifice for the beauty of your message, America's message. Let's all join you. Let's make this an Oscar-winning, Cannes winning majestic effort. Jesus, Valery, God has made this evening, this collision of purpose happen here. Right here, if we have the heart to seize the day, the night, the moon and all the stars. If we have the heart."

Spradlin wondered, *American Message? Real Estate Aggrandizement? Valery's incredibly lithe and oil smooth long legs throttling your torso? Her back and forth trapeze swing into and out of lust's sweating hands and strained forearms?* Spradlin admired Lem's efforts to wring cash out of passion, both patriotic and petting.

"Your buddy seems about to pull all the stops out," Dr. Nasr said to Spradlin. "But I didn't back a film, I bought a speculative option on land ownership, with a guaranteed return."

"The film's maybe the key to the land," Spradlin said, somewhat amazed at his slide into selling. What's Florida but Hollywood on slow steroids? A finger rammed into Caribbean eyes."

"What's that supposed to mean?"

"See the film and realize what's more important than even Rumi's verses. More significantly, help Lem round up Russian investors."

"I've landed radiologists from Orlando/Tampa down to Naples and up to Tallahassee. Buzz has appellate lawyers from Jacksonville to Key West all owning options of Longboat Key, if everything pulls together. And when Johnson wins his war in Asia, we'll all settle for rents of beloved Longboat Key, with the Sailor Circus performing every evening as part of the jewel of the renewed Ritz-Carleton on the Gulf." Dr. Nasr said.

"And now Lem is pulling in patriots to the trough. Is the deal so sweet or is it just a con, a mammoth Ponzi scheme with early backers paying for latecomers?" Spradlin asked.

"Nobody's paying anybody yet. It's all a monster option play with a pretty good chance to pay off amazingly." Nasr said. "That's how land deals play out here in crazy Florida. Maghribi had words for it: *You are a drop, speak not of the ocean./ You are an atom, speak not of the mighty Sun./You are of today, speak of today;/Since you know not of earth and sky/Talk no more of above or below./Since you do not have musical talent,/Speak not of tune or tone,/Go beyond No and Yes, my son* . . . options on beachfront land are beyond No and Yes. Russians and fervent anti-Communists will keep the game afloat. Lem will take us all beyond fear." Nasr laughed.

"Beyond fear and into the sweet arms and legs of blessed Valery." Spradlin said.

"Speak for yourself alone," Nasr added.

And indeed Lem, his arm around Valery's shoulder, evidently dazzled her with whispers of moonay for her film in the relic hotel. She seemed intent on disengaging, but found Lem's weight and perhaps his message difficult to put aside. Then quickly as Valery swiveled Lem patted her left buttock and slipped his pinky just a fraction inside the lip of the tight edge of the sheared denim. She turned back to him, smiled and pulled away. Lem turned to the three Russians elders who moved close to watch. Valery melted into the crowd around the microphone.

Later in the drive back to Longboat Lem announced far too loudly, Spradlin thought, "We're invited to the set—to watch Valery and Steve do it in the hotel's gazebo. Can you believe it? Just after some sunset when the light's perfect. Don't you get? Showing the movie will be the perfect conclusion to our gala celebration of the Longboat Key Preservation Trust. Maybe at the hotel itself, if we can find a caterer with our kind of vision."

"Our kind?"

"Okay, my kind of vision. Have it your way, right up until you see cash, boat loads of cash heading toward me, toward us. Some Russians will come in. I feel it."

"But no commitments yet?"

"You learn in the moonay game never to press when it seems opportune. Always let the mark set the time schedule. At least that's what the books say."

"You read about fund-raising?"

"There's a literature on capital investment, venture capital. But reading about it ain't nothing like doing it, and, Johnny, we're actually doing it. I can't wait to wade into the next revenue stream."

When they got to the store there was a police car at the Peverill house. "Maybe they found her body," Lem said.

They sprinted across Gulf of Mexico Drive and Chuck Stover met them at the front walk. "A mild robbery, guys."

"What's mild?" Spradlin said.

"Not that much taken. No big items. Maybe a couple of pots, one closet worth of clothes, and some game boards. Course you're never sure until you get a full listing. Sometimes it takes days before a loss is noticed and more importantly recorded."

"No forced entry?"

"Back slider wasn't locked. Probably came in that way. No forced entry. You're right. The girls are a bit upset, so I wouldn't bother them. I got all I need to get things started, but I suspect it won't go much of anywhere, anyway."

Marlene came out, "They got my watches, three of them, and some clothes and Birch says some stuffed animals. It's pretty weird, maybe pretty scary, isn't it?"

"Not the usual run," Stover said, "must have been watching the place."

"That's pretty creepy. What am I supposed to do? Pack heat?"

"That's a great idea," Stover said, "Turn Longboat into a shooting gallery. That's all I'd need."

"I wonder what do you need, anyway? I take it you still have nothing about Tine. Isn't that so?"

"Without a body I'm not sure what I can do. Or anybody else either."

"Would a reward help?" Marlene said more gently.

"We could try it. Post something in the store, maybe. Put something in The PeliKan, if it's still publishing." Stover turned to Lem, "Is it?"

"We're working on it," Lem said. "When it comes out, I'll run something. How much of a reward?"

"Reward sucks," Marlene said. "Let's can it." And she went back inside.

"Well, she knows her mind," Lem said.

"We've got a thief with very special inclinations." Stover said, moving toward his cruiser. "Probably a pervert. That's where I'll start tomorrow. 'Night, boys."

After Stover had pulled away, Lem waved to him muttering, "Goodnight Scoutmaster Chuck, you fucking hay-seed. Lunch pail asshole."

"How unkind," Spradlin suggested.

"Let's go see Jimmy and get him to set it up with VanShuten."

It turned out Jimmy was not in much of mood to set up anything. He met them in his yellow plaid robe and resisted opening the door further. So Lem made his pitch from outside, with tree frogs pronging the night air, and at least three bats circling Jimmy's roof.

"You've got to set us up to meet with the VanShuten. We heard you know him. We need access to him for a variety of reasons," Lem said hurriedly.

"Well, one anyway," Spradlin added, "money."

"He's lynchpin," Lem continued, "loaded and with connections all over the West Coast. With him on board, the whole deal sells itself. The backing will be majestic. Just what you wanted, Jimmy. Exactly what you specified. You can make it happen. We've got to talk to him."

"Fellas, it's late. I'll consider it tomorrow. Right now, goodnight."

"Goodnight, Jimmy," Lem said with over-drawn sweetness.

# Chapter Six

In the next few days Spradlin opened the store more and more often. It seemed to him that it wasn't simply that Jimmy wanted to sleep late; something else was going on, keeping Jimmy at home. When Jimmy did come in, he seemed tired and drained and distracted. Authority somehow had washed out of him. Jimmy stopped talking about improving the building. The rain-holding pails seemed heavier, the stains on the wall board elongated, and there was a striking absence of chiding toward Charlie Dyer or Earl. Even Spradlin could occasionally retreat to a stool near the registrar. The ambience of the store radiated cereal box rather than rotisseried chicken. The Place's message seemed evident: "Nothing is cooking here, so stock up on staples and leave quickly."

For Spradlin the one bright spot came when Birch and Marlene came across Gulf of Mexico Drive. They had taken up Tine's habit of a daily morning trip to the store. Dyer was, as always, delighted to engage with them, if occasionally that seemed to annoy Marlene.

"Is Jimmy at home again today?" Birch asked.

"The Lord prefers his manor," Dyer answered. "Nobility has its prerogatives."

"Tine used to say there was something royal in Jimmy's manners," Birch said.

"Jesus!" Marlene commented.

"Would you ladies, like a personal delivery of your goods today? It's the slow season and I have time for attendance to all your needs."

"We'll handle our own baggage," Marlene said. "But you can tell us what Captain Stover has found out about Tine's 'disappearance,' if anything."

"Nothing, my lady," Dyer said.

"He ain't been by in a week," Earl said from behind his counter, "The last I heard he was going down below Venice to ID a body washed up there on the Gulf. Pretty chewed over."

"Jesus!" Marlene added.

"Earl, spare the ladies the details. Theirs are instinctively tender hearts. Let's respect that, acknowledge that for what it is."

"And what is it?" Marlene asked with enough snap to back up Dyer a bit.

"Only to say your toughness has an instinctive glove kindness."

"A glove kindness, doubtless white glove, and demeaning." Marlene continued. "As if we're just slobbering embarrassment over our own 'disappearance.'"

"Charlie's only trying to recognize our worth, Marl. No need to upbraid," Birch said.

"Marl disagrees. Marl sees only your instinctive (yes!) relapse into subservience, genteel acceptance of a subordinate role, a slimy acceptance of patriarchy. I'm astonished you junk your credentials before these buffoons."

"Buff—foons?" Earl said incredulously from beyond his counter.

"Yeah! That's a multi-syllable for ass." Marlene said.

"Okay, I get it." Earl said. "It's what you think."

Marlene seemed non-plussed by Earl's admission. See went back to the front of the store and got a small metal carriage and eased it into the cereal aisle.

Spradlin consciously rearranged his sneakers on the stool's bottom rung and marveled at the colloquy.

"I'm here to help, if you need it," Dyer said lamely as a closer.

Marlene was still leisurely wandering the aisles when Jimmy came into the store. He perfunctorily greeted his workers and turned to Birch. "These fellows giving you any trouble?"

"No," Birch answered, "not me. Maybe Marlene."

"I can't sort that out just now. I'm supposed to help Rev. Ward for his 'soft opening' of the revival. I just stopped in to make sure we're fully staffed and taking care of our best customers."

"We'll be just fine," Marlene called from the paper goods section.

"Steadiest customers, anyway," Earl said.

"Steadier than you, that's for damn sure." Marlene said, coming to the meat counter. "How about a pound of baloney to have with your baloney?"

"Of course." Earl said.

"These fellows talking baloney to you, Marlene? I can't quite believe it. I'll see to it they speak only truth and politely." Jimmy said.

"Give it up." Marlene said.

Jimmy laughed, turned and shouted for Spradlin to join him. "We'll walk the beach to Bainer's rehearsal. You need a good baptism, John." And together they crossed the road and took the narrow path beside Tine's house to the slanting Gulf beachfront. The slant made side by side walking difficult, so Jimmy took the lead speaking to Spradlin over his shoulder and slowing his steady stride as his statements became more studied.

"The sun's baptism enough," Jimmy said. "We can ignore Bainer's invocations, can't we? On the other hand, the notion of baptism isn't so bad is it? New beginnings, starting over, striking off in new directions. Learning that everything you've begun should be jettisoned, isn't that the message we need to experience? If you can't learn it, it simply pounds it into your crumbled brain, isn't that so?"

"If you say so."

"It's pounded into my brain. Striving is never arriving. Never arriving. Always pausing to collect various organs of you spilling out on the hot sand, trying to round them up and stick them back inside your open side. Blood darkening the damn hot sand. He was writhing around, hands and fingers stoking through the dark sand from his own blood, pulling at tissue, bone fragments wedged oddly in the dry white sand sparkling like laughter at his desperation. John, you know why I was shown that? What was my witness supposed to, supposed to do? And sunlight just like this. Why? Should I ask Bainer that?"

"Great idea. But pick up the pace a little. I'm running up on you."

"We couldn't have that. Picking up the pace is always better than understanding why we're walking to the rundown trailer park, and its rundown preacher."

"I don't think he's rundown."

When they came to the stone jetty about 100 yards before the Trailer Park Beach, Jimmy decided to go out to the flat rock extension that terminated the artificial barrier doubtless put up in some hope that the structure would hold the beach against hurricane erasure. "It's like an arm trying to gather up or maybe shield the beach from outside savages."

"Man-made grace against the elements," Spradlin said. "Maybe a natural fulfilment of what you saw in the Philippines when that soldier tried to collect himself . . ."

"While I kicked him, and others did too. 'Shitty fucking animal,' they called him, kicking him. They really thought he was an animal. I didn't think that."

"Pretty pathetic animal."

Jimmy sat down on the rock and Spradlin stood behind him so Jimmy could lean back against his shins and knees. Looking to the right Spradlin could see perhaps ten residents of the trailer park sitting in green canvas chairs on the beach in three groupings. Momentarily he thought they were bushes. The sunlight was so bright, and the salt air seemed to defuse his focus, but the green was too bright, too unnatural and so the white plastic armatures materialized holding creatures overdressed in windbreakers and sweaters despite the October warmth—emblems of native Floridians mystified that Yankees could swim, and wanted to, in the apparent chill. Presently two technicians appeared among the groups and put up poles with narrow rectangular speakers mounted on them. Sound boxes Spradlin imagined for Bainer's messages. And true enough, presently Bainer's resonant voice came wafting out of the boxes:

"Incline your ear to my cry, for my soul is full of troubles, and my life draws near to the grave. I am counted with those who go down to the pit . . . you all getting it?"

Flannel-clad arms went up into the air, apparently signaling affirmation.

"I need to hear it from you!" the boxes commanded. And a cheer went up.

"Great!" the boxes replied, then added, "Mason, you got the reading for this afternoon? Maybe push it up a tick or two. There'll be more bodies on the beach later. Otherwise stay with the reading."

Jimmy said, "I've heard enough. Amplified Bainer is no better than Grocery Bainer, we can go back. Thanks for the back brace." Jimmy turned to the left and lifted himself by yanking on Spradlin's arm.

But Ward's voice over the speakers came alive again: "Oh, you can't go, Jimmy. You can't go. I've seen you, and now you must come down to the park on the beach. If you leave now, I'll come after you. We'll all come after you, and that will be embarrassing, unhelpful, perhaps shameful, but lately I'm thinking that's an overworked, over-used word. Don't you agree? Shame has no standing, does it? No standing. Like you: standing but without standing; Just something stupid blocking, temporarily, the sun. So come down here and we'll have at it on the beach. In full view of this discerning audience. A theological shootout in the sunlight, with the cameras recording it all. Get your sorry ass down here now!"

Spradlin wondered if Bainer was somehow closer to them than the audience now standing in front of their green chairs and looking around. Maybe the sun was in their eyes? More likely they were elderly and suddenly put off by Bainer's crude term. Jimmy was upright but seemed woozy, off balance, and tentative. So Spradlin took hold of Jimmy's right shoulder and aimed him away from the edge of granite cliff. "You okay?" he asked.

Jimmy yawned and seemed even more tottering. So Spradlin guided him carefully toward a path back off the jetty.

"Coward!" screamed the boxes. "Come down on the beach and meet your better. You can't leave me alone in the pit. Why do you hide your face from me? Your fierce wrath has gone over me. Your terrors have cut me off. They came around me all day long like water. They engulfed me altogether. Loved one and friend you have put far from me, and my acquaintances into darkness. And I alone am here to heal you. Make you whole again. You cannot leave me, locked as I am in your heart."

Jimmy tottered again, rubbing the heels of his hands into his eyes, then bringing his palms slowly down his face, then squinting and slowly jerking his head left and right. As if regaining solid footing, he said to Spradlin, "Tell that asshole narcissist to go to hell."

Spradlin answered, "Only after I get you back to the store."

2.

When they did get to the store, Earl and Dyer were playing cards on top of the meat carving block. The store was empty. The game ended as soon as they saw Jimmy.

"Get some chairs from out back," Spradlin said. "Jimmy needs to sit."

Dyer sprinted away. Earl put the cards in his apron pocket and asked, "What happened?"

"Nothing happened. Jimmy's just feeling woozy, right Jimmy?"

"Yeah, woozy. Maybe nauseous, more than woozy. My head's killing me."

"Jimmy's head," Dyer said pushing one of the white plastic arm chairs he had retrieved from outside under Jimmy's back. Jimmy settled onto the seat. "Jimmy's got a hurting head," Dyer said, coming around front and bending down to look at Jimmy's sagging face.

Marlene muscled Dyer aside. She leaned in and held her left forefinger in front of Jimmy's face. "Track my finger with your eyes," she said softly but with a professional authority that impressed Spradlin. She moved her hand back and forth and then said, "He's okay. He'll be okay. But take him to an ER."

"Too far," Jimmy said through a wheezing breath.

"Then you need to take some aspirin right now. Right here. Get water and aspirin. Take three."

"Did he eat something there?" Dyer asked Spradlin.

"We didn't even get there, much less help Bainer."

"We could put him in the truck and take him into Sarasota," Dyer said.

"Whatever she wants."

"Who cares what she wants."

"She used to be a RN," Spradlin lied, and that seemed to persuade Dyer. In a half hour they drove Jimmy home and arranged him on his brown couch so that he could see through the sliding screened panels to his lanai pool glistening in the late afternoon sun—a ridiculous iridescent blue shimmer.

"I'll stay here a while in case you want to go the ER," Spradlin said. "Maybe we walked too far up the beach."

"Yeah, too far." Jimmy said quietly. "He was wiggling, writhing on the sand, blood leaking everywhere. His intestines looked purple and slimy, really, really slimy. The slimiest thing I'd ever seen. He kept snatching at them, trying to put them back in. But he couldn't. I could have told him that. Should have told him that. 'Look, fellow, too late to reassemble . . . too damn late for that.' Anybody could see that. Anybody could have told him that. Why didn't we?"

"No sense shutting the barn door now," Spradlin said, "You can't put the toothpaste back in the tube."

Jimmy half sat up, staring at Spradlin, then squinting at him while breathing harder and harder. He pointed at Spradlin and wheezed: "You are so fucked up," then slumped back on the couch coughing as his left leg spasmed and clamped rigid to the tired, foam middle pillow.

Dyer ran back to the truck and drove to the store, returning with Marlene and Birch.

Jimmy was no longer talking, and it seemed his left side had frozen somehow.

"Jesus," Marlene said, "a stroke. We've got to get him to the hospital. We'll take him in Birch's car. You and Charlie go back to the store, keep it open and running."

At the store Dyer said, "Stroke's the worst. Comes lickety-split out of nowhere. Nowhere at all. And leaves something frozen, done for. Something unexpected, like a paralyzed organ or something terrible."

"We don't know anything." Spradlin said.

"We know stroke's the worst."

"I thought people recover from it."

"Oh, recovery comes down the pike, but never quite gets home, never back to level. Not level. Not solid again. I can tell you that 'cause my daddy had a stroke and never got swallowing back."

"What?"

"Couldn't learn to swallow, lost swallowing. Couldn't take food. Couldn't get it down. Tube down his throat till he couldn't stand it. Tube to his stomach till he couldn't afford it. Nobody around him could keep it up. Wore the mixer out zizzing up stuff to pump into his stomach. Wore everybody out trying to feed him. For what? He talked like a five-year-old. Lot of jokes about poop. He starved to death."

Spradlin listened in amazement. "I don't think Jimmy had a stroke."

"Maybe he didn't and that'd be a blessing, a veritable deliverance, but I'd be worried whether we deserved such deliverance."

"You don't, that's for sure." Spradlin said.

"You're too judgmental, Johnny. Seems Jimmy Faneuf doesn't deserve incapacity and so we'll hope along that line. But consider the possibility of a stroke, turn it over in your word-spearing mind. And repent your dastardly tongue." Dyer chuckled.

The store's absolute quiet continued customerless till closing at 8:30. Phone calls from Birch revealed only that they remained with a half-paralyzed Jimmy in the ER still awaiting treatment. Spradlin took the cash drawer back to Jimmy's house and then drove to the hospital.

He found them on a corridor just beyond the ER. Jimmy was on a gurney against a brilliantly orange painted cinder block wall. Birch was hovering over him and at the same time fending off Marlene's objections.

"The residents," Marlene said with emphasis on the slurring nature of her designation, "the residents gave him blood thinners—standard protocol or so they said with, get this, 'potential stroke victims' as if they were unsure of his condition. So of course, let's wheel him off to the corridor so that when a bed opens up, we can do an accurate diagnosis. Better yet, letting him wait in the corridor might just kill him, solving all our analysis problems. Jesus!"

"Marl. . . ." Birch said.

"Fuck you. He could die out here and what good would your little girl triage sentiments do him?"

"I don't even know what triage means."

"Of course you don't know since not knowing is your forte. Little girl who learns everything and leans forever on Daddy to solve the little dilemmas of this life."

"Gratuitous shit," Birch answered.

"Gratuitous but right on target. Poor little rich girl who had everything but love and who let the world know it. She just couldn't settle for that. It wasn't natural, was it?"

Spradlin thought, *is a stroke a natural dilemma,* but said, "is Jimmy having a stroke?"

"Let's ask the assembled physicians," Marlene said. "Oh, there aren't any, are there? Gee Willikers, what shall we do? Maybe pray. Yes, all together pray for the priest-physicians to come. Wouldn't that help most? You go first. You seem like a perfect date for miss little 'debutante from Shaker Heights, in her first life crisis. Let's see how she handles it.'"

"Shut up, Marl. Jimmy needs our help."

"Seems like he doesn't need any help. Dying's straightforward . . . helpless."

Spradlin felt a strong grip on his right shoulder, turning him out of the way to the gurney and a soft voice saying: "In my annihilation is annihilation's annihilation. And You are found in my annihilation." Spradlin tore free of the grip and saw it was Dr. Nasr moving between Birch and Marlene. Although no one had asked, Nasr said by way of explication, "Mansur Hallaj, 1173 or thereabouts . . . My most effective low volley." He smiled at Spradlin.

"Dr. Nasr!" Spradlin shouted. "Jimmy's had a stroke."

"We don't know that yet," Nasr answered.

"Left side's paralyzed," Marlene said loudly. "They're giving him blood thinners. But the damage is already done."

Nasr began wheeling the gurney and he said apparently something in Persian as the wheeling picked up. "We'll take him to the ICU and some imaging."

"How?" Spradlin asked.

"I'm on call and when I heard it was Jimmy Faneuf, I came because we need Jimmy, don't we?"

"Apparently," Marlene said.

"We all love him," Birch said emphatically.

"He whom Love has passed by/ Is a wingless bird, unable to fly. —Rumi, maybe 1251 AD," Nasr said.

"Left side is wingless all right," Marlene added. "Fucking wingless. Poor Jimmy."

"Not so poor, if Lemuel is to be believed," Nasr said, smiling.

"What does that mean?" Marlene asked.

"Nothing," Spradlin said. "Lem knows nothing . . . has only dreams."

"Were you to catch, in a cup, a sea, / How much will a day's portion be?" Nasr offered as an explanation. "Rumi, again, 1251 or so. And now I'm at doors you cannot enter. Jimmy will be fully restored." And he leaned to left, whacked the metal square plate with ACCESS stenciled on it, so that the doors opened inwardly. He eased the gurney in and did not look back as the doors closed behind him.

3.

At the end of four days' visiting Spradlin believed Jimmy would not be fully restored. They had moved him out of the ICU to a separate room, without a roommate. And Jimmy lay on the crisp starched sheets watching the blank olive-colored screen of the T.V. on a pipe from the ceiling and about three feet from his inert forehead. Most mornings Spradlin sat in the black faux leather side chair reading the Sarasota Herald Tribune and listening to Jimmy's regular breathing. He left Dyer and Earl running the store and figured they mostly argued since the regular customers passed through by 10:30 a.m. and there were few tourists in early fall.

At the end of the first week, Jimmy's sister, Agnes, came in from Iowa to take up the watch for, she said, "No more than five days since I have a family you know, too, unlike Jimmy."

In every way Spradlin found her substantial, a hefty beefy woman in a ruby colored shift who spoke softly but had a way of pushing aside any deterrent to her plans for Jimmy's transfer to a rehabilitation clinic. Dr. Nasr thought that premature, but she found an ally in her brother especially after he began speaking slowly, slurringly, but distinctly enough to side with her.

"Agnes . . . is . . . right. I . . . want . . . to . . . go," Jimmy said to them both.

"Save it for Dr. Nasr," Agnes answered softly. "Keep your strength for when we'll need it. Can you bend your legs?"

Jimmy shook his head. "Maybe . . . right . . . one. I . . . need . . . to . . . put . . . the . . . other . . . one . . . on. Why . . . won't . . . they . . . let . . . me?"

"Don't worry. I'll speak to them. They've got some protocol that stipulates the time for reattachment. Makes little sense to me, but I can negotiate something. Don't worry about it."

"Thanks . . . so . . . much. You . . . always . . . take . . . care . . . of . . . me."

"What goes around, comes around. You always protected me." Agnes said.

Spradlin wondered what she needed protection from. He thought of Nasr after tennis intoning a Rumi poem: He whom Love has passed by/Is a wingless bird, unable to fly . . . Spradlin wondered to which of the Faneufs the verse applied. Watching the sun baked parking lot with its sparkling chrome spears of flickering light he imagined for some reason bounding bears thundering toward a five-year-old Agnes with Jimmy simply motioning them to the side, so that the torrent upended cars but left a ruby-clad, scared girl untouched. Maybe it was only one very large bear.

But she wasn't at all scared in telling Spradlin, "Some stroke victims imagine a part of their body has floated away. Spend too much time hunting around for it, if you can believe what I'm telling you. Our first job is to convince Jimmy he's whole with maybe a part that has fallen asleep. So that's our job, once we get Jimmy free of this system." She motions to the room. "I can count on you. I know that. Yes, indeed, you are my ace soldier in this rescue. We'll get Jimmy back his life, you can count on that. I can get Jimmy going. That's my role in his life. How do you think he got to Florida?"

A further ally in that quest to get Jimmy going turned out to be Lem, who came to the hospital on the third day of Agnes' visit, and just at the moment of her most confrontational argument with Dr. Nasr. Spradlin was amazed at the low-key sparring between sisterly concern and expertise's authority. Just when it seemed expertise would triumph and Nasr prevail, Lem aimed the sparring elsewhere.

"Look, Irv," Lem targeted Dr. Nasr in a way that stunned Spradlin, "Getting Jimmy whole again quickly serves all our interests. Serves them best. The important thing is that Jimmy is operative and fully cognizant of his commitments. That's what has to be achieved here. Jimmy incapacitated puts a hold on everything, fouls up everything. An unwell Jimmy frustrates everybody. So we have to risk letting Jimmy and Agnes show us the way out of this mess."

What impressed Spradlin was that the equality of the tennis court apparently carried over to a hospital setting in which a doctor and patient's advocate could plunge ahead on a first name and hectoring basis. Mentally Spradlin tried out "Look, Irv, enlighten me as to my double wonder: what Agnes needed protection from, and what 'mess' you and Lem have cooked up."

Instead of asking those questions Spradlin listened further struck by Nasr's capitulation: "Okay, I set it up to move him to a rehab clinic somewhere. It's not so damn easy setting up a transfer."

The only word Jimmy said in the hospital's transfer van was said slowly with, apparently, a conscious equal emphasis on each syllable: "Fil . . . i . . . pino."

"Yes, yes, Jimmy, of course there may be Filipinos to help you at the clinic." Agnes smiled at Spradlin on his bench on the other side of the gurney. "He's always fond of Filipinos, always talking about them. Even on Longboat Key?"

"Once in a while," Spradlin answered, "mostly about a Japanese prisoner there. Wounded and putting himself together."

"I know all about it," Agnes said. "Everything, every single detail." And she turned to Jimmy, "They'll help you get your leg back, but you'll have to work hard at it. It won't be easy, Jimmy. It will require focus and effort, lots of effort. And most of all, persistence. You can't give up. You've got to get yourself entirely back. Don't you want your whole life back?"

Jimmy grimaced while trying to nod his head. It seemed he'd bitten his lip.

"I wouldn't push too hard," Spradlin said.

"I leave in two days. I've got to push. Got to get him going and going well."

"I'll be here and so will Charlie and Earl, and Birch and Marlene. He's got lots pulling for him."

"And that's a blessing, but I've got to know he's on track for full recovery before I leave him, so whether you or they," she motioned toward the rehab campus, "like it, I've got to push the pace. I want to see him walking before I leave, so let's make that the initial goal. I know how crucial the earliest full commitment can be in eventual success."

When they got to Abyssinian Rehabilitation Pavilion, she pushed to have Jimmy attempt a walk into the open lobby. But the technicians politely insisted no such deviation from protocol could occur until the patient was entirely settled into his room. Even then they passionately argued for Dr. Nasr's presence before any regimen be undertaken. Agnes ignored their entreaties. She asked Jimmy to step off the gurney and walk to his bed. She pulled his legs off the gurney and offered to brace him, if he would ease his buttocks off the thin, narrow cushioning. When he did so he collapsed into her so that she motioned to Spradlin to keep him upright. He yanked Jimmy away from her, but it was clear he'd have to grab him to keep him upright. They wobble-walked him to the hospital bed.

"See what we're talking about," one of the technicians said to the space above Jimmy's head.

"I get it. He's not ready," Agnes conceded.

"We get, that a trained therapist should be in charge, and calling the shots," the technician said.

"Point taken," Agnes said. "Thanks for all your help. Please let Dr. Nasr know Jimmy's room number." And when they had left, she continued to Spradlin, "Give a dog a little authority and it goes to their head, doesn't it? We don't have to be lectured to by such youngsters, do we?"

Before Spradlin could answer a large, tall ink-black woman wearing lime green scrubs came into the room and threw her hefty arms around Jimmy and hoisted him into his bed and set about getting sheets and blankets around him.

"We'll set him up, and in the morning get him walking. Go home now. He'll need you tomorrow. That's important. Doctor will be by later after we get him set."

## 4.

In the morning, when Spradlin arrived with Agnes, Jimmy was up and moaning, and wavering, and moaning, and falling back against the bed which seemed cranked up to a difficult height.

"Take a step to me," Agnes said. "Take a step. Just one."

"I ... can ... not."

"Horsefeathers! You certainly can. You just won't. I told you it would be difficult and a long road. You've got to stay focused and working at it. No time off. No leisurely imaginings that life could be different, or more accommodating. It cannot be. From now on it's a fight every minute, every day, every week. But you can get back. You can be Jimmy Faneuf again."

Jimmy swiveled against the bed, turning away and said quietly, "... why?"

"Oh, don't start that game again. We've been down that road, Jimmy. And you know where it ends, don't you? Of course, you do. I'm here. I've come a long way to get you set up again. Let's just focus on that task. Straighten up and take a step toward me. Make that stuck leg work. Make it now. Just will it into a step."

Jimmy slumped forward on the bed, resting his head on the gnarled sheet and blanket forming something like a pillow for his right ear.

"I wonder who set him up," Agnes said. She joined him at the bed and managed with Spradlin's help to get his legs up on the mattress. "Oh, my sweet brother, rest. We're not here to torture you. Rest. We have time. I have time. We came to help, not to hurt. Rest a while and we'll get started later. John, go get yourself some coffee. Take your time. I'll sit here with him. We have time."

"You're a woman of mercurial moods," Spradlin said.

"Don't be a judgmental dipshit. Go get your coffee. I'll need you later."

"A . . . nice . . . shot . . . Ag." Jimmy said, shifting a bit on the lumpy blanket.

And Spradlin turned over that assessment in the lobby of the hospital, before a nine-foot waterfall over obviously papier-mâché rocks, into a blue vinyl immense pool. He drank two tepid lattes.

Presently Dr. Nasr and Lem joined him.

"I can tell you his health is good. Blood pressure fine. Heart beat solid. Blood thinners doing their work. But he resisted Rumi's declaration. Utterly resisted it."

"And what was it?" Spradlin asked smiling.

"Oh, some verses from *The Eye of Outward Sense*: . . . Your foot stands not firmly till you move it,/ Nay, till you pluck it not up from the mire,/When you pluck up your foot you escape from the mire,/ The way to this salvation is very difficult./When you obtain salvation at God's hands, O wanderer,/ You are free from the mire, and go your way . . . Agnes liked it, but Jimmy not so much. I think we'll actually have to rely on the therapists, the pros. They have a steadier game and stronger serves, better low volleys. You get the picture, and maybe Agnes will."

Lem added, "True help is on the way. Bainer said he was going to stop by, so that a true disciple and a true God could work His magic. And we truly need Jimmy to sign in his right mind, and sound body, with total control of his faculties, don't we?"

"I'll let you fellows sort that out." Nasr said nodding and leaving.

"What are you talking about?"

"Saving The PeliKan, by giving it land and prospects and backers . . . investors with real stakes in Longboat's future, its preservation and development. Our life work, Johnny. What we came down to this finger of possibility for. We can make this the true Other West Coast. Out of the mire as the good doctor says."

"I'm not in for your latest hair-brained dream," Spradlin said.

"You don't have to be. In fact, you can't be. It takes mazooma to get aboard this train, and I know what your worthless net is."

"And you've conned Dr. Nasr to back you."

"Not just Dr. Nasr, a covey, a gaggle, a fucking herd of doctors from Siesta, and Casey and Venice and Naples and even Fort Meyers—mostly dentists—who dream big to bring Longboat into the times. The golden times of real estate price acceleration. They're at the trough and by God we're going to feed them. So we all cleanup."

"I'm not in."

"You are if I let you, and I'm going to let you. You'll thank me a thousand times when this giant clam opens."

"Yeah, full of your paste pearls."

"We'll see who wears them at the biggest ball of all. Even Uncle Waldo wants in, even Evelyn, if you can believe it."

"And Jimmy is a lynch pin?"

"Jimmy makes it happen," Lem assured. "But I've two more constituencies to tap. One for mazooma, one just for *in kind*. So you and Bainer get Jimmy prancing. I'm out for final collections. Wait till you see what we've got planned. Ciao, and fix Jimmy. Fix him good!"

"And get him to sign . . ."

"Nah, just to make Agnes happy and heading back home. Getting her the hell out of town."

For a moment Spradlin warmed to Lem's enthusiasms, but soon enough recalled Lem's constant delusions. When Spradlin got back to the room, Bainer and Agnes were deep in conference while Jimmy lay inert on his bed.

"Pray with us," Bainer directed, but Spradlin stayed in the door jamb. "Lord," Bainer shouted, "look with favor on this child of Yours who for so long nourished the down trodden of Longboat Key and who through constant effort kept food on the tables of the dispossessed and disabled. . . ."

Disabled? Spradlin thought.

"Who more than fed the lonely and the heartsick at his store—the very way station of solace for all the residents of Longboat Key. . . ."

Residents? Spradlin thought.

"Heal him, Lord. Heal him! So that he may walk again and worship again and celebrate again Your bounty and grace. . . ."

And sign, thought Spradlin. Yes, sign, Lord, get Jimmy to sign! Would that it were true, thought Spradlin.

"We humble ourselves and seek comfort in the folds of your majesty and in the supreme confidence of your healing properties. . . ."

Properties, a term Lem understood, Spradlin thought.

"Send down your radiant spears of wellness so that your humble servant Jimmy can talk quickly, and walk quickly, and continue his tireless work on behalf of the ill, chastened, and sadly grieving folks of Longboat Key . . ."

Who's sadly grieving? wondered Spradlin.

"Render him whole and prosperous so that his beloved sister may believe in his future. . . ."

And ours too, investors all, thought Spradlin.

"Knit up his pain, infuse new life in his muscles, new joy and anticipation in his heart so that the work he has so manfully begun. . . ."

Manfully? Thought Spradlin, or spears of wellness?

"Do not leave him in the Pit, Lord, cast away from human commerce, from those he loves unable to walk to them, unable to salve them in their own pain, so consumed is he by his own. Unable to console his loving sister who has come from great distance to aid him and who despairs of his rejuvenation. Grant him, oh Lord, the strength to pry his leg into striding, his heart into thrilling anticipation of a future so bright as to blind the sun. Only you, Lord, can, through the blink of an eye, fashion a new world for him and all of us. . . ."

Doctors and Dentists and whatever other constituencies Lem was hauling in, thought Spradlin.

"A new world bright with promise, full of your grace and abundance . . ."

No more trailer park thought Spradlin.

"Full of your resonance and in perfect concordance with your commands, so that, yes, he might kneel before you, yes, we might join him in kneeling and profound reverence for the glory of your achievements so evident in simple striding you grant to him and to all of us."

Simple striding, pen in hand, Lord, thought Spradlin.

Bainer had taken a kneeling, near prostate position, but now as if lifted up, rising and suddenly in terrific decibels began chanting: "Heal me oh Lord, for my bones are shaking with terror. Oh Lord my God I cried to you for help and you have healed me. Bless the Lord O my soul who forgives all your iniquity, who heals all your diseases who redeems your life from the Pit, who crowns you with steadfast love and mercy." Suddenly Bainer stood up, backed away from the bed and shouted at Agnes and Spradlin: "Why do think evil in your hearts? For which is easier, to say, 'Your sins are forgiven,' or to say, 'Stand up and walk,'? But so that you may know the Son of Man has authority to forgive sins—Stand up take your bed and go to your home. Jimmy, stand up! Stand up! Stand up! And go home! Now, Jimmy, now, stand up! Stand up!" Bainer's voice spiraling into thunder, "Jimmy, stand up! Stand up!"

As Agnes and Spradlin watched Jimmy's right leg shifted to the edge of bed and then eased off, dangling for a moment. Then the left leg joined in the motion and Jimmy robotically came to a sitting position.

"Jimmy, stand up! Stand up! And go to your home!"

Jimmy eased forward, slid toward standing on the floor and for an instant stood upright as if to step off toward his home. Agnes flashed an amazed smile toward Spradlin instinctively moved backward to give Jimmy more room.

"Yes!" Bainer shouted, "Yes, go to your home!"

Jimmy blinked and began to step forward when suddenly he pitched toward them, clearly falling and at the same time making a harsh growling sound that culminated in a full vomit tossed directly on Bainer's shoes, as Jimmy crumbled to the grey linoleum.

Moving to the side to avoid any of the spreading puke, Spradlin thought—Lem's connection to VanShuten is going to be delayed.

# Chapter Seven

It turned out Jimmy's connection wasn't needed. Three nights later Spradlin and Lem were invited to a rehearsal at the ghost hotel, and Gary VanShuten was there too. He stood before a Pennzoil rental truck that had improbably crashed through Longboat's mangrove brush to the one open space before the hotel's broken entrance. VanShuten and Valery were laughing with, Spradlin thought, entirely too stilted, indeed manufactured, joyous laughter.

"Are you really gonna do it in the empty gazebo? On what? On a air mattress?"

"That's where Noah says we'll end up, but it's going to be a disrobing by levels till we reach the top and the music spins us right into it. All of it. It's great. Steve goes down on me for a good while, and then I reciprocate. And then we spin together till we're spent. It's in the script." Valery's eyes flashed as she watched VanShuten respond to her itemization. "Noah's a super professional. Steve's got a great body."

"People won't be watching Steve," Lem said.

"Don't be so sure," Valery added.

"Lemuel's correct, as always," VanShuten said shaking Lem's hand. "Nobody will take eyes off of you, my little lithe one."

With envy Spradlin fixed on the possessiveness of VanShuten's phrasing. He drew slow, delicious breath, savoring the word *lithe*. He imagined how mesmerizing her legs entwining him might be, how breath-stopping, how bubblingly ecstatic her undulations beneath, above, below, or beside him surely would be, how frenzied their tip-toeing on the mica edge of slurping surrender would have to be. And then the deepest dark dive into the sweetest, slipperiest vault of long tantalized, now gushing, liberation. Tear this scab off again and again, sweet Valery.

To ease his desire Spradlin lamely said, "Can I see the script?"

Valery pointed to the grey notebook a very skinny tall fellow was holding by the truck's passenger's door. "Let him look, Noah."

"It's not a script, just a series of story boards. You know plates of what could happen," Noah said. "Sometimes we adhere strictly. Sometimes we veer off. But mostly we get back on track. I did the story boards."

VanShuten said, "The lights are in place. Let's do a strip up the stairs. No camera, just a run through to make sure things come off on schedule."

"Steve's upstairs someplace checking out elevator shafts," Noah said. "We'll have to wait."

"The Hell we will," VanShuten said. "Valery can take us through without him. I'm on a tight schedule. Let's go! Imagine a long kiss and get going up the steps. What comes off first, the skirt or the blouse?"

"Obviously the blouse," Valery said, smiling and mimicking a lengthy passionate kiss with an imaginary Steve. Then on each cement step Valery unlatched a button of the excessively frilly white blouse. By the fifth step the blouse slipped off her shoulders and began a descent toward her waist."

"Jesus!" VanShuten said, "Bra won't work. Either no bra, or better yet a lavender camisole. Yes, camisole. I like camisole."

Lem said, "Sounds like a slave auction," and he moved directly toward VanShuten, who in trying to watch Valery moved away, closer to the steps. But Lem kept crowding him, and Spradlin wondered momentarily if Lem was pushing toward a confrontation.

But Lem clarified the situation, "Mr. VanShuten, I've put together a consortium to preserve Longboat Key and a number of supporters have said you might be interested in coming in. And your presence on the supporting list would guarantee success——"

VanShuten pulled away and kept staring at ascending Valery. "The bra now. You're on the ninth step and almost turned away from the camera slash audience——I'm on any number of lists. Too damn many lists. Why should I want to be on yours?"

"Not so much a list as a group of like-minded investors who want to keep Longboat from turning into Fort Lauderdale."

"How will that make me money? ——Valery, I don't think you should drop the skirt. He should pull it down. Don't you think? We're seeing passion here, aren't we? Where the hell is Steve? I'm not a tree hugger. I didn't save a single oyster in my life. Swallowed every damn one of them."

"We're not talking water quality. Just the orderly development so Longboat looks like Siesta or Casey keys after development. Not like the Lido or Miami." Lem persisted, "I want folks to see your concert hall. Not shrouded with tall condominiums."

Noah shouted, "Okay Val, just shimmy it down, push it down yourself. Kick it away on to the patio. Nudge the bra off the ledge at the same time. We'll match the music. There's towel on the edge of that level. Lie back on it and imagine Steve chowing down. He'll ease the bikini undies down himself. How does that look?"

"Valery, you look just great. Really great! Maybe we should carpet that ledge." VanShuten said.

"Absolutely not," Noah added with surprising emphasis. "It's the image of the loss of loveliness in the whole setting, the corruption and decay of Ringling's dream, that's what I'm after. I want the immediacy of Valery's flesh, young vibrant bodies, in contrast to the sad disintegration of the building. That's the whole of it."

Spradlin wondered what 'it' was.

VanShuten turned to Lem, "How much to get in?"

"Fifty K."

"And what's the return?"

"For the first year, ten percent guaranteed, but if you stay in, hundreds of percent."

"I doubt it," VanShuten said, "But if you guarantee ten percent for the first year, I'm in. Speak to Amory Boyd for the wordage.—— Valery, I could watch you all day, yes, all day indeed, but I have to get to Tampa by noon, so I'll look to the final cut—probably with Steve. Right?"

Valery stood and wrapped herself in the lime green towel.

## 2.

On the way back to the store Spradlin turned to Lem and asked, "Tell me about your 'consortium'. Is it like your 'backers' of The PeliKan? Just what area of cloud cuckoo land does your 'consortium' occupy? Did you just make the whole thing up?"

"At least I have ideas. And I've got backers—doctors and lawyers. I don't do sarcasm. All that cloud-cuckoo land stuff. I don't do mockery."

"But you do, do fraud."

"You can look at it that way. Losers often do. But risk-taking is the essence of success. And that's a lesson I doubt you'll ever learn."

"I wouldn't get too insulting. I might be your only visitor in jail."

"What I like about VanShuten is his absolute directness. He knows he's taking a chance and he's prepared for it, 'cause he knows the payoffs can be magnificent. And what's more he's got a commitment to keeping this area full of God's natural grace, despite the tough guy exterior. He knew exactly what I meant about Casey and Siesta Key and Miami. He knew what he wanted to avoid, just as I do. We're on the same channel. It's terrific. I can keep working that channel for all the moonza around here."

"But the ten percent per year comes from where?"

"From the next investors! Right down to the moment when a federal grant for the environment picks up the game and launches us into another bracket. It's dicey but every dare is dicey isn't it?"

"Thank you, Phil Ponzi."

"I don't think his first name was Phil. And besides the environment is the real payoff. The good guys keep the bad guys from developing Longboat. And if ten percent doesn't quite materialize, preserving natural beauty will suffice, especially for the kinds of assholes I have for backers."

"They should hear how you talk about them."

"They won't care. Ten percent return covers all disappointments. But more importantly the dream of really hitting it big will overcome my slander, which, incidentally confirms their admiring view of all real estate speculators. If I didn't talk tough, who'd believe me? Even you succumbed."

"True. You conned me into The PeliKan."

"We had a dream, and the best part is, we still do."

"Oh, bless our dream." Spradlin said, as they pulled into Jimmy's store.

There were no customers. Earl and Charlie were sitting behind Earl's counter.

Lem said to Earl, "The bird ready?"

"Ready a half hour ago."

"Not too dried out?"

"Juicy sweet. Just like Deborah likes it."

"Okay. Come along, John. You'll get to meet my main backer."

"Deborah Kohl?"

"Who else? She's got the second biggest slice of Longboat. And it turns out Earl has been bringing her roast chickens since God knows when."

Earl said, "Yeah! But you actually got in."

"Earl was always left at the doorway. He doesn't have my charm."

Spradlin said, "Nobody gets into the Kohl place."

"That's right, nobody. No body. Just me. Come along, Johnny. I'll show you how."

They parked along the right edge of Gulf of Mexico Drive outside the mammoth wrought iron gate. There was an oak door beside the gate through which they entered. At the main door Lem pressed a yellow button and hollered into a speaker. "Hi Deborah, it's Lemuel with your chicken from Earl. Today's meal, darling."

Presently the carved hickory front door eased back about 12 inches. A bespectacled small freckled face appeared around the edge of the door. She was wearing circular steel rimmed glasses and seemed fascinated by her feet, or perhaps the parquet floor.

Lem pressed ahead, "Deborah, this is John Spradlin, my assistant. We've got your bird, so you have to let us in. Please back up a bit so we can get in."

"The papers, my magazines," she said. "No room."

"I can get enough heft to move the pile. Not to worry. John can help me. We can move the pile." Lem signaled to Spradlin and mashed his left shoulder into the door. Spradlin came around and rammed his left shoulder into the door too, achieving a space wide enough to enter. Deborah had backed up and was now standing on a two-foot high stack of magazines.

"Please don't damage the newspapers. I haven't read them that year." The news print stack was seven feet high. There were four such stacks like sentinels before the left parlor room. Spradlin noted there was a slender passage through the stacks, if you turned sideways. He noted there was furniture in that room, but the two couches and the three heavy arm chairs were weighted down with stacks of newspapers and magazines, and in the case of the largest arm chair, pots and pans filled its wide cushioning, on top of which were three stacks of National Geographic Magazines. The floor was littered with felt hats of a variety of shapes, a wash of purple velvet sea.

"Where are we eating today?" Lem asked with a buoyancy that signaled some sort of game.

"Oh, where do you think, this time?" Deborah answered.

"Looks like a trail left open on the stairs. Should I take it?"

"Beware of tigers," Deborah answered with excitement. "They haven't eaten in months."

"So, they're too weak to be a threat?"

"Just like everyone else," Deborah said.

"So, I'm going up. Follow me, John, but be alert."

Books stacked four feet high filled each end of each marble step.

"Don't knock anything over, John," Lem said. "And when we get up there which room for the perfectly cooked bird? Earl's burnt offering."

"Oh, not a room. Just put her down on the next to top step. That way when I need to read something while eating, everything is nearby. And tell me some news of the wider Longboat world. I know it's passing me by."

"Yes, indeed." Lem said, "Tine Peverill still hasn't turned up. No body found. Her sister, Birch, thinks Chuck isn't trying very hard. You heard anything? Health Dept. been by lately?"

"Oh, you can't bait me, Lem. No, you can't. You know they wouldn't come by unless someone complained. But there's no one to complain."

"There always someone to complain," Spradlin said.

"You have a rude friend, Lem."

"Oh, he's not rude, just a little dumb. Means well though and can be helpful lifting things." Lem said. "He's a partner too. Can you believe it?"

"Can't," Deborah said, "Doesn't look to have means. Or did he just barter his lifting instead of actual investment?"

"You're always too sharp, Miss Deborah. You size up my world flawlessly. But despite John's appearance he has some family connections—always a plus in the investment world, isn't it Miss Deborah? And those relatives saw, as did you, the certitude of my plan and the wisdom of our offering. Yes, indeed even though John here hasn't the means he had the connections. They cottoned to what we've noticed and planned for. And they came in for almost the same share you've designated, without the enormous collateral you've tossed into the effort. You needn't worry that your voice won't be instantly heeded in the decision process sure to unfold in the next sixteen months. No worries there, Miss Deborah. None what so ever. You sure you want the bird left on this step? Seems an awkward place to eat."

"Oh, it is, but look around you. Where else could you eat? I filled the place up. And now three self-storage units, too, in Bradenton."

"Climate controlled units?" Lem asked.

"Of course. We're in the semi-tropics, didn't you know?"

"Of course, I knew. It's John, here, who gets confused."

"And will be eaten by tigers, no doubt." Deborah said giggling.

"No, John won't be eaten alive. He's too agile for that. You can watch him back down the stairs. Very agile fellow. And we'll come again next week and best of all with your bird I'll bring your first dividend check. Won't that be swell?"

But she didn't answer. Merely stood on her magazines and looked longingly across her crowded rooms. The hoardings were impressive. Hats and coats, strangely labelled boxes—cardboard with neatly printed black marker designations: Paris, 1948; Dublin, 1953; Salad Tea Bag Tags; Now, 1964. Beyond the book-lined semicircular staircase there was a wide hall leading eventually to something that appeared between boxes and stacks of more newspapers to be a kitchen, and at the very entrance to that tiled room on the floor was a small air inflated mattress.

"You still got your bed upstairs filled up with stuff, don't you Deborah?" Lem said.

"I sleep downstairs now. The stairs are difficult except for food on the penultimate step. You know about that phrase don't you Lem?"

"I live it every day," Lem said. "You sure the Health Department hasn't sent someone to check on the place?"

"No one has complained, no one knows." Deborah said.

"The dead bird knows. Each week she knows." Lem answered.

In exiting Spradlin thought of Rumi's lines: "Keep silence, that you hear from that Sun/Things inexpressible in books and discourses./Keep silence, that the spirit may speak to you . . ."

Before the car started Spradlin asked, "How much is she in for? And what about her relatives?"

"They're more skeptical," Lem said. "But she's in all the way, with a home equity loan bigger than the moon. The relatives are not happy, but they are compliant, especially if we dangle some access of their own, sans investing moonza."

"I don't see how it can work."

"You just keep agile, finding new revenues, new investors and then there's truism about real estate: Johnny, they're just not making any more. Per force, it appreciates, just like we do. Per force, appreciation. Believe me everybody wants and believes in it. Everybody. Every single body. So, think about the resurrected PeliKan. That lovely bird just soars— no, cruises four feet off the tide water, scooping occasionally whatever she can, until the Health Department declares the place a hazard, a terrific hazard. Down come the golden walls. In comes the emerald sea. Away we flee to that noble country without any extradition . . ."

"You flee. I'll stay behind and savor the outrage."

"Suit yourself," Lem said. "I can imagine you wallowing in the wreckage. Tonight, come along and hear how the Russians see the venture."

"Maybe how would-be Hollywood has been conned, followed by wealth's widow among hazardous waste is enough vision for me. Rumi says, 'Imagination is paltry indeed to conceive of such/ A Sun as he is beyond imagination and intellect.'"

"Whatever that means." Lem said. "Rumi would be surprised how I can milk anti-Communism out of its cash, and its longing for memory's majestic world."

"Rumi would not be surprised."

"But you would. Believe me I serve up a delirious mix of traitors in the bushes, and acres of real estate to re-establish the world they remember. I talk to them about Sikorski floating his company on mythical bonds to declare that all was not lost, even after it had been lost. Resurrection's the only powerful myth left. You can get it all back. You suffered unimaginably but you can get it all back. Intoxicating vision. You remember the soft afternoon on the lawns of sweet green feelings; your women in pearls and white; your children speaking French with their tutors and playing with innumerable things. Dazzling sunlight not quite equal to Gulf sunsets but stirring old longings. Yes, it's all there for retaking, resurrecting life itself. I tickle that precious core of longing that palpitating sponge of heartache for what was and might be again. It opens a gash in the side, sluicing out cash, endless cash for the past's undoing, or re-doing. It takes just one taking the leap, and soon enough others join in. The declaration of joining soothes all unacknowledged hurt. Funds flow in as heart sear torrents toward a new St. Petersburg on the Gulf. The Longboat of triumph over Soviet desecration and now blessed Romanov restoration."

"Well, you've sold yourself."

"The very first step of success in this American world. A lesson you've never learned, and never will. You're the pathetic wilted child of ironic doubt. You'll never get shut of it."

"But I'll stay out of the slammer."

"Check with me in ten years." Lem said.

# Chapter Eight

Lem made weekly visits to Jimmy's store through the late fall and into the "season" of snowbirds' descent on the west coast of Florida. Spradlin imagined Lem needed to touch the groceries or feel the cool glass of Earl's counter just to renew his strength for continuous solicitation for the preservation of Longboat Key. As far as Spradlin could tell, not a single investor ever came from Lem's strolling visits through the store. Doubtless too many "lunchpails" littering up Longboat's trailer grounds, Lem complained to Spradlin.

There was a certain irony in Lem's remark since Spradlin thought "lunchpails" now ran the store. Jimmy had recovered most his voice, but his mobility was restricted. He had difficulty walking. So, he came in less and less. Spradlin understood enough about re-ordering and Earl had some sense about balancing the contents of his meat counter with the contents of the walk-in meat locker. Dyer always had suggestions and some of them, Spradlin found, made sense. But the store lacked Jimmy as center and Birch and Marlene did not compensate for the disappearance of Tine. But business held up; tourist traffic increased and the required distance driving to better stocked groceries worked in Jimmy's favor. There was residual loyalty to Jimmy, reinforced by the failure of rumored grocery chain stores to materialize. Lem told Spradlin to spread stories of rattle snakes and periodic flooding among customers so as discourage Arvida-like acquistors from competing with him. Spradlin countered with speculations that rumored rabid animals hardly stemmed demographic growth all around Sarasota Bay.

Increasingly Spradlin found it discouraging to bring the cash drawer to Jimmy each evening. Invariably Jimmy told him to sit down and recount carefully who had come into the store and what that day's purchases needed particular restocking. Those recitations were tedious enough, Spradlin felt, but he found Jimmy's questionings about what had happened to his body more troubling, and eventually irritating.

Each night Jimmy replayed watching the hapless Japanese soldier's writhing on the sand of a Luzon beach. Each night Jimmy walked Spradlin through his questions of justice and faith concerning what he assumed was some deity's will concerning the event. "I keep remembering how he clawed around searching for some piece of intestine, some glop of blood, to tuck back inside of the appalling cavern of exposed stomach and lower intestine. I kept hearing a voice shouting—'why aren't you helping? Why are you just watching and feeling unbalanced, lurching, as each groan whines its way to your ears? Why not kneel down and push things back in? What's holding you back? Your buddies' nervous laughter? Or some stupid sense of cleanliness that would defile you by handling such an atrocity? Or some sense that the enormity of the agony exposed was simply beyond any imagined rectification. Yes, that might have been it. Couldn't that have been it, John? What paralyzes us, John? What?"

"I don't feel paralyzed."

"Good for you, John. You walk easily, too. At your age everything functions fully and joyously. Jesus! That's luscious! My feet feel numb, or sometimes they feel tingly and my back feels like some unkind soul has put a five-foot icepick through my right kidney down my right leg to my frozen right foot. Getting out of bed takes an hour, a full hour to get dressed, getting first one foot, then the other through the openings in my briefs, then each pant leg pulled up. Jesus! John, why can't we kneel down and put that poor fellow back together?"

"Maybe because twenty years ago he died on some Filipino beach, and we're not there now, are we?"

"Why aren't we?" Jimmy said each night. "Why aren't we?"

2.

In April just after Easter, Lem began poster publicity for what he called "Longboat's Preservation Evening"—a celebration of the island's longevity and a public presentation of a master plan from the Longboat Investment Group for the key's future. Preserving natural and idyllic "environmental moments" appeared to be the central goal of Lem's investment group. But the appeal was cross-generational. The poster for the celebration featured bare breasted Valery sprawled on the top level of the first-tier stairs toward the skeletal gazebo on the ghost hotel's roof. Through the vanished wall spaces the Gulf in resplendent blue/green held a boiling, roiling golden red sunset with ghost-white cloud wisps steaking the sky.

On the Friday before the great celebration, Lem gave Spradlin his most compressed spiel, "Yes, the movie will go on in the background on a huge rented 25 by 14-foot screen, brought in from Tampa. But the kicker is that simultaneously with the showing, Valery and Steve and small band will re-enact the movie live. So it will be double vision for the audience—hyper 3-D, the living screen at work." Lem smiled.

"VanShuten insisted on the live show, I'll bet," Spradlin said.

"Yes, but it cost him another share of the partnership, since it's practically a private show for him."

"And five hundred others presumably."

"Oh, more than five hundred. I've got a food boat tied off the backside. Earl's whacked a five-foot track through the underbrush so the multitudes can walk down to the water and get finger food, kid stuff, and desserts. Maybe bars of hazelnuts and chocolate."

"And Port-o-lets?"

"Five of them on the walkway. Shouldn't that be enough?"

"I guess you'll find out."

"And an architectural contest with posters so that the best future renditions can be chosen, with prizes and runners up rewarded. And Longboat Key magnets offered for under three dollars each. Real metal, even with topographical ridges."

"Ah, the Longboat mountain range somehow depicted."

"Yeah, but without any reference to volcanic activity."

"And never a high tide."

"You sound like my father. He refused to come in. Flood fear, hurricane fear, tsunami fear, what have you."

"Is he right?"

"We'll know in 50 years."

"God willing."

"God's nothing to do with it. Only investing partners now and mother nature. But as distraction/attraction; the two are united utterly in any selling experience. There'll be a 40-foot table piled with near endless long sub sandwiches, Italian only. So, all you have to do is pick up a knife (conveniently left at five-foot intervals) and slice off a chunk of the sub for your personal sandwich. And a second table full of Fanta Orange soda cans. Large paper napkins only, just the chance to traipse about the Hotel ruins and chomp away on a dreamy sandwich, sans choice of ingredients. Italian only. Get it? Of course, you don't get it. You're still hung up on choice, deluded about choice, bemused by choice, rendered inert by choice. But you'll see how choicelessness is intoxicating. Come down on the day and watch. While you're eating, two smaller screens will continuously show a vision of Longboat down the line. Maybe something like Longboat 2050, or 2100. Streaming gleaming condos spearing upward in a silken blue sky. But straight ahead the crowd gets to watch Valery and Steve in the flesh ascending the naked-making stairway toward the golden gazebo on the vacant roof, pausing for slow fornication at each tier of the journey, and beyond them, exact jumbo version of their frail living bodies on the mammoth duplicating the action on the ascent. A double whammy of titillation—VanShuten's dream, precursor to his purple concert hall anchored in the bay. And the side screens detailing a Longboat of pristine, immaculate minimalism or an island full of residential towers filled with the elderly warming themselves on narrow tiny balconies in their own sunlight of nasty intentions. Elderly eating grapes and inhaling sunsets of spectacular swirling red-orange billows."

"A Longboat of bow and arrow hunters or at the same moment ancient, creaking daiquiri drinkers, on faux leather recliners, oiled and sweating in the sunlight." Spradlin added.

"Mockery never sells, never succeeds, don't you understand that?" Lem said. "It makes you, and no one else laugh. It pleases you, and no one else. Nada. Total loss. If you can't get beyond it, you'll never get anywhere."

"Here we are."

"Very funny. Chuckles galore. But how many partnerships did you sell this day? This week? This month? Ever? But the real issue is how much publicity can we do for this opportunity? How far to go to get the right sort of potential investors? How guarantee they'll step up to the plate?"

"Valery will show them what's necessary, what needs to get done."

"I don't think you know," Lem said slowly, pridefully, "that the film students, actors, crew, technicians came in for two partnerships. Who would have thunk it? I did, because I know what enthusiasm can engender—what pockets it can suddenly open. Aspirations drive investments. Daddy was right. He also says the damn subpoena is only an invitation to negotiate. But, Johnny, you only know hesitation and doubt. And worse yet, mockery. Pure loser."

"Tell me about your damn subpoena."

"Not now. Not on the very precipice of success. It's all coming together. When the few who have made the pledge, taken the plunge, begun to see returns beyond measure, when they circulate among those still thinking about coming in from the un-aspired land, from tentative dreams, from dreamy longings, from vague hopes to direct action, with checkbooks in hand; when they come in, then we can address the so-called legal issues."

"We?"

"I plan to rat on you," Lem laughed. "Don't worry. Nobody conceives of you breaking any law anywhere. Your listless incompetence has saved you from all retribution."

"But not apparently you. What are you planning to do?"

"I'll know best, after I do it. But don't worry. I won't implicate you, unless, of course, I have to."

"Fuck you!"

"Haven't you been with me on every foray? At every venue? Sometimes haven't you even spoken with soft, sweet persuasiveness?"

"Fuck you!"

On the day of the great event—Longboat's Preservation, Lem chided Spradlin again, even as the crowd started arriving, "We'll let the grand jury sort things out." Lem laughed. "Now, see even the lame have come here to partake." Lem gestured toward Jimmy slowly working a walker between Dyer and Earl.

"Well, Lem," Jimmy said, "You've got them parked on both sides of Gulf of Mexico Drive from the bridge to John's shack." Jimmy gestured to the crowd now pushing into both sides of the long, long table. Knives flickered in the late afternoon light as slices of the endless sub sandwich were chewed away. "No chips? Big mistake. They'll start chewing on the napkins."

"Simplifies cleanup."

"Makes a crude sense, Lem. You've got acres of people here, and no kids."

"Town fathers previewed the film and said, 'mature only.' Also, kids don't do full partnerships. A kid couldn't have done what you did, Jimmy."

"I'm beginning to regret throwing in with this crowd."

"Oh, they're so much better than the non-local investors. They're all in."

"And all promised ten percent return for the first year."

"The Trust makes regular payments and the charts are up in St. Armands. Everything's kosher."

Jimmy smiled, "So when's the show starting?"

"Poster viewing is open now. Check the pillars and the ends of the open stairs. Noah will announce the food ship is open for drinks and boxes of fried chicken, if you want more than the sandwich."

And as if on cue Noah's loudspeaker voice stormed over the mangrove bushes and washed through the standing cement remnants of the truncated hotel: "Captain Charlie has dropped the 'Longboat Forever' banner, and that means the food ship is open for real drinks. Rewards stronger than Fanta orange. And also, food beyond slices of sub sandwich. So, stroll down and look over the various student posters of Longboat's future. And get yourself some real libations and wander back for the spectacular show beginning right as the sun starts to set. Sample a bit of what John Ringling dreamed about: what could have been, what would have been the West Coast's most glorious, most wondrously proportioned hotel, a jewel worthy of this jewel key. Will that long dream finally come to fruition? Only the Longboat Trust can decide that. And who is the trust?

You're looking at them! Yes, all of us here have partnered to save this glorious key, to preserve this key, this way of life from the suited swine profiteers who are raping Florida's golden green heritage. Yes, we've come together to insure something so wonderfully natural and bountiful will be preserved for generations, through at least our grandkids. Isn't it so? Yes, we've taken steps, opened our wallets, pledged our savings for this island, this way of life, this freedom from exploitation and the ravages of profiteering. We're fashioning a plan and future. Together we'll rediscover John Ringling's greatest longing— for a verdant key on the most blessed coast of all of America. So let's celebrate together tonight. Let us dream together tonight. Let us together prove that orderly thoughtful development and reasonable cash return can sup together, as we do tonight. As we dream together, enjoin together to preserve natural beauty and white sand soft surfaces for our grandchildren, let's still keep the Trust growing, expanding, leveraging its successes toward more success. We mustn't stop now, not till we have brought The Ritz-Carleton Hotel of Ringling's dream home to its cared-for mangroves and glorious beaches. Welcome to the newly preserved Longboat Key! Now wander down to Captain Charlie's for real refreshment and check out the poster visions of this magnificent key for tomorrow and beyond. When the sunlight darkens a bit come on back to the lobby of this wondrous lost hotel and we'll start the film with the stars of tomorrow: Valery and Steve. Show time approximately 6:30, but we'll ring a bell so you'll know. As you walk, folks, listen carefully, thoughtfully, for this blessed key is saying Thank You for its preservation. Take care and above all enjoy it all, revel in its extraordinary beauty. Revel, too, in its exceptional possibility."

Noah put the microphone on the truck torn grey fabric seat and came directly over to Lem,

"We had to cut most of the C and F from the film. It freaked out the City Commission. Gary insisted on showing it to them. Really idiotic I told him, but Gary does his own thing. Ned spliced over the excisions pretty well."

"C and F?" Spradlin asked.

"Cunnilingus and fellatio." Noah answered quickly, quietly.

The sandwich-sated crowd moved almost as a unit slowly through the battered lobby and on to Earl's cleared track to the distant beach and Captain Charlie's floating bar. Squeezing on to the track forced so many together that their heads seemed a rippling wave of brown hair, brown darkness, streaming toward the Gulf.

"They're like lava," Jimmy said, shifting his walker slightly.

"An unstoppable force," Lem said, "Even Arvida's terrified of them. And well they should be. Popular will is supernaturally strong."

"Popular profit," Spradlin said.

"Profit's hardly evil," Lem insisted, "It keeps the crowd together. It makes a common value. Let's move to the improvised Green Room behind the shards of the reception desk foundation. At least we can sit there before the show starts."

"You never want them sitting. Sitting leads to thinking and thought's the enemy isn't it?" Jimmy said. "Thought's the death of grocery buying, and real estate too. Isn't that so, Lem?"

"I never challenge your wisdom, Jimmy. Takes time from finding additional partners. Know any we haven't touched?"

"I think there's a colony of Jehovah Witnesses near Clearwater, or maybe they were Seventh Day Adventists," Jimmy said, smiling. "I heard you got the whole Russian community."

"Absolutely did. As well as the Birchers and the Freedom ringers, when we promised there'd never be fluoridation on the key."

"Ah, the Longboat Dream: No fluoridation, no sewerage, a refuge for rabid species from all over Florida, and only soybeans and kale grown without fertilizer." Spradlin said.

"Jesus! John! Let it go." Lem sat down on a large blue tarp that covered what must have been an oversize, heavily cushioned couch. The couch was behind the concrete substructure of a vanished reception counter. Beside the couch were four folding chairs.

"This had a marble top, one long piece. But it got snatched in the late 50's. Pretty amazing it lasted that long. Course, there was a lot of growth then, and I'm sure it was heavy. Picking it up would have popped the guts out of an average guy." Jimmy said.

"Was Earl working for you then?" Spradlin asked.

"Probably. I don't keep employee records."

"Neither does Earl. Doesn't have to." Lem said. "I hope Captain Charlie has the staff to handle the glut."

"If he doesn't, we'll know soon enough."

Noah first and then Valery and Steve wearing enormous, butter-colored Terrycloth robes, came around the concrete wall behind the couch. It seemed they were naked under the robes, but Valery corrected that impression, "Do I leave my panties on or does he rip them off?"

"There's a cosmic question," Spradlin said.

"What did the fucking City Commissioners say?" Noah asked.

"It wasn't clear," Valery said.

"So let's just leave it unclear. Do what you want."

"It's a mutual artistic decision," Valery persisted.

"Art was driven out of this mess," Noah said. "Do what you want, whatever the moment desires. Whatever . . ."

Valery thought for a minute then turned to Steve, "At the third landing, rip them off."

"Got it." Steve said and from his robe's pocket he pulled out a bottle of Michelob, drank it furiously and tossed it aside. It spun of the concrete platform adjacent to the vanished counter.

"Art died," Noah said, "the minute real estate investment took over. I thought they could be unified. Sex sells property, somebody said that, the way sex sells everything, and I thought maybe you could usher in a double-edged crescendo, an orgasm of signing on the dotted line, so to speak. But what a fucking educational process this has been. Art and commerce never mix, just like somebody said, some ancient time ago."

"Long ago, that's a cosmic expression," Spradlin said.

"Fuck you," Lem said. "Give up your fucking sarcasm. And besides the whole damn mole army is coming back. We better give them what they want." He pointed to the slow-moving brown mass slowly rippling back on Earl's track.

"Places!" Noah shouted, "Leave the robes on. Projection! Get the titles on the main screen. Get the future visions on the side screens, but hold the titles. Freeze it, so we can tease them a bit and wait for more darkness."

"Real darkness is at least an hour away," Spradlin said.

"There's good cloud cover," Noah countered. "We'll do."

Valery and Steve stood preening on the first step of the circular rising stairs. Spradlin liked the way the stairs spirally leisurely toward the next floor. The steps seemed like massive tongue depressors arranged in clever ascent. The brown mass muttering and occasionally laughing loudly slowly filled the lobby. Bodies against the pillars. Bodies ascending the stairs until they were called back by Noah's technicians. Very bright lights flicked on illuminating the steps.

"Look fascinated by each other," Noah shouted. "Begin wooing now."

"Wooing? Really?" Spradlin said.

"Fuck you," Noah countered with a muffled voice. "It's okay to kiss, but lightly. The sun's still too damn bright. Light necking."

"Necking? Really? Where did you go to Catholic high school?"

"Fuck you," Noah said a bit unmuffled. "That's it, Val, maybe a bit of the robe off the shoulder. Get set to run the film.

Get set! Keep the crowd off the stairs. We're approaching lift-off. When I signal, Val, drop the robe. But only my signal. It's got to be keyed to the projection. Your run and the film have to fuse. Have to fuse, or as close as we can get to that, but not yet. Get ready for my signal. Kiss more deeply."

The crowd seemed to hush, having apparently caught on to what might happen.

Over the growing quiet, Noah bellowed, "Projection!! Now, Valery, Now!"

Both robes flowed downward piling up around their feet. Steve entirely naked kicked his robe off the stair ledge. Valery simply ran upwards out of her robe, flesh color panties nearly transparent and a visible, stunning confirmation of her long red hair. She sprinted up the steps. Theatrically Steve lunged after her, reaching for the back of panties but deliberately missing. Identical film depictions appeared over and beyond them on the large screen; simultaneously the side screens switched to full color projections of Longboat Key of the immediate and destined future. Tall condos pushed off from rich, green mangrove bushes. Steve caught her on the second tier, encircled her and pressed her for a well-rehearsed nine-second kiss. The crowd burst into applause and that instant celebration drown out what Spradlin thought were police sirens coming onto the key. Valery broke away and sprinted to the next tier just below the concrete Gazebo. Steve gained on her and together they plunged onto the strategically placed air mattress. Steve tossed away her panties. The crowd cheer reached thunder clap proportions. Valery's legs unfurled skyward toward the Gazebo as Steve mounted and thrust at first slowly and then with more crowd-cheered swiftness. Spradlin was aware red strobe lights were coming through the jungle growth out to Gulf of Mexico Drive. The filmic version was intensely confirmatory—penetration was occurring on the screen at the least. But such audience inquiry into whether it was witnessing a double experience was savagely interrupted by the swiveling red lights of what seemed a stream of uniformed state police.

A bull horn silenced the cheering: "This party is over. OVER! Disperse immediately. IMMEDIATELY. Anyone remaining will be arrested. This party is OVER!"

There was a momentary, head-whipping-around moment as if the crowd would have to make a simultaneous decision. That moment seemed elongated as floodlights suddenly flashed onto the Gazebo and from its center a short white sheathed woman came forward to the extended lip of the roof. With a slowness either of over-theatricality or, more likely, aged decrepitude she elevated her arms, trailing the wide white sleeves like some imagined geisha and flicked her hands outward as if scattering invisible confetti on the brown mass below.

"Good God!" Jimmy shouted, "It's Tine Peverill!"

But the spot lights flicked off and in the blinking aftermath she disappeared.

# Chapter Nine

The next morning at the store Earl said, "Was it Tine? I couldn't see well enough. Light too bright. Too much noise. Cops. Sirens. Blinking blue lights. Somebody said it was Tine."

Jimmy said, "I don't think so. How could it be? It's been nine months since she disappeared. Besides, Tine would never pull such a stunt. I can't imagine her stepping in front of even a small group and the idea she'd take the top floor to show off in front of a huge crowd is absurd. Just absurd." Jimmy moved his walker toward Earl's counter. There was green plastic chair at the end of Earl's counter and when Jimmy came to the store, he invariably sat in it.

"Aren't you afraid of doing a 'sitting down kind of business," Spradlin said with some enthusiasm as Jimmy sat down.

"Did you think it was Tine?" Jimmy asked.

"Of course he did," Dyer answered from the front doors. "He's got the best eyes of all of us."

"So why don't you let him answer?"

"He knows his place. I can answer for him." Dyer said.

"That's right. I know my place and old Charlie always can answer for me."

"I know it was Tine. I'd know that woman anywhere. I'd know her in a second. Those hands." Dyer said and disappeared into the front cereal aisle.

"So where is she now?" Jimmy continued. "Where? Hehn?"

"Maybe she was just an apparition, or some projection from Noah." Spradlin said, "We should ask Noah. I bet Noah can explain everything."

Suddenly Charlie reappeared at the end of the paper goods aisle, "Maybe we should just be happy we got to see her one more time. She's a heavenly vision, isn't she? Isn't that enough?"

"Why don't float that theory by Birch?" Jimmy persisted. "Or Stover? I bet Stover would really embrace that explanation."

"She was, and is, a vision," Dyer said. "That's good enough for me."

"I don't know if you can take a shower for a vision," Spradlin said.

"I can indeed!" Dyer answered.

"Self-gratification, wins every time."

Dyer shouted, "Earl, teach sonny to watch his tongue." And Earl came out from his counter; Spradlin moved quickly to the register. "Just kidding, Earl, just kidding."

The Tine speculation/evaluation stopped. At noon Dyer said, "Jimmy, I'm gonna take the truck, and me and John are getting' lunch up in Anna Maria."

"There's no place to eat in Anna Maria," Jimmy said.

"Oh, you don't know everything. Place is developing like crazy. You ought to get off slow Longboat."

Jimmy nodded, "Sure, Anna Maria is a happening place."

When they were in the truck, Spradlin said, "Jimmy's right. There's no place to eat in Anna Maria."

"Oh, there's one place," Dyer said. "And that's where we're going."

In silence they drove past Longboat Trailer Park, past the longest stretch of overgrowth on both sides of Gulf of Mexico

Drive, past The Diplomat Apartment complex, the first and only development on the key, past the Colony Beach Club Yacht Basin and finally over the bridge to Anna Maria. Suddenly there were small bungalows and shacks with tin roofs. Spradlin thought the area was a movie set for some epic about "Fishing villages" in some southern area of India. The closest entity to a town center was the juxtaposition of a laundromat and gas station. Dyer turned the truck down a narrow road that quickly became unpaved and dusty, passed further through a near-embracing mangrove thicket and came eventually to a yellow double-wide trailer resting on cement blocks about forty feet from the most northern turn of Sarasota Bay. The water sparkled in a subtle tide ripple but otherwise had a brown cast to its color. Spradlin thought, there ought to be bare-breasted Asian women hurling nets into the bay.

"Is this where you live, Charlie?"

"Is indeed. Home and hearth, little fella."

"In a doublewide?"

"Unlike any doublewide you've ever seen in your very limited life."

"I never thought of you as a doublewide guy."

"I never thought of you as such a simple shit. Now let's see what's for lunch."

The earth outside the truck was spongy, turning wet and soggy in their steps to the trailer. There was a thick moss covering the stones Charlie had put down before the narrow aluminum door. Spradlin needed the door edge in his hand to keep from slipping. The door opened directly into a kitchen and there was a short woman in white slacks standing at the small refrigerator, her back to them, as they came in. She turned around, and it was, indeed, Tine Peverill.

"So it was you last night at the hotel"

"Oh, that was Mister Dyer's idea and Noah's. They thought it would be dramatic, but I knew it would just be silly, especially so after the police arrived. Wasn't that dramatic! Why did they come?"

"Something about pornography being filmed on the property, love." Dyer answered from the doorway.

"Does Noah film pornography?" she asked.

"Apparently so, love."

"It's hard to separate art from pornography," Spradlin said still stunned to see it was Tine Peverill. "Have you been living here the whole time? I mean while everyone was searching for you."

"Yes, the whole time. Does that seem difficult for you?"

"Well, yeah. Yeah!"

"I told you, love, he doesn't have much imagination. She thought you'd be different. Maybe more understanding."

"Don't be so chiding, Charlie. I've spoken to you about that. Put some fences around what you think. Let's have some chicken salad. I've worked all morning on getting the tarragon flavor just right. It's Charlie's favorite. He thought you'd like it too. And after lunch we'll take a walk and I'll explain everything, won't I, Charlie."

"Explicate it like a dream, love. Only you can do it. Isn't that right, sonny?"

Spradlin didn't answer, pushed his way past Tine to the narrow Formica- topped table set up in the living area of the doublewide. Three yellow chairs, one at the end, one on each side of the table had been set up. There was a crystal bowl of chicken salad in the middle of the table. Plates at each place held two matching slices of seeded rye bread. There was a small bowl of what appeared to be mayonnaise near the chicken salad, although it looked already overdressed with that condiment.

"I don't think we can just pretend everything's normal, so the happy couple invite a friend to lunch." Spradlin said.

"Oh, of course not," Tine called from the kitchen. "You want milk or tea?"

"How about we skip the libations and provide some explanation." Spradlin answered.

"In due time," Dyer said. "Don't you know you can't hurry a woman."

"Jesus! Why all this coy shit? What's going on?"

Tine came to the table, put three tall, iced, tea glasses down and then sat opposite Spradlin, "Make your sandwich, and learn to listen."

Spradlin stared at the crystalline chicken salad, thought about getting up and walking out, maybe back to the highway, maybe out into the brown bay water, but eventually he picked up the orange handled spreader and shifted some of the salad onto the bread. He then looked into Tine's grey-blue eyes in a way that signaled, he imagined, he was ready to listen.

"We worked it out on that first beachwalk," Tine said. "Charlie proposed that we just keep walking, maybe running away. Just leaving. Leaving everything. It was he said," and she smiled at Dyer, "just like closing the door and heading north, never looking back. Never. That seemed dreamy, really dreamy. Of course, it was just a silly notion. I think Charlie proposed it just to spook Earl. He believes in ghosts, you know. We kept refining the idea walking to the hotel, and we both forgot about it, didn't we, while we were exploring the hotel, which incidentally was really scary and precarious."

Spradlin wondered if scare and threat motivated her.

"We decided that after the hotel tour, Charlie would propose a swim to cool off. Maybe even a skinny dip," she giggled. "Before we went back in the truck. We'd swim out in the Gulf and Charlie and I would keep up a conversation as we pulled further and further away from Earl. Charlie would keep up the chatter even after we got so far out Earl might not be able to tell what was going on, but he'd be reassured everything was all right."

"And he was reassured. He heard love in our conversation," Charlie said smiling. "Love and splashing about"

"I'd keep swimming back to the Kohl's dock. It was just a joke to fool Earl, who's such a sweet simpleton."

"Sweet and mean," Spradlin said.

"Now, sweet and very concerned. I guess we didn't plan on that, did we Charlie? We thought it would be such a good joke. Fooling old sweet/mean Earl. Charlie would start yelling that I had gone under, and there would be searching and lots of despair. But we didn't figure Earl would keep looking for so long, keep diving past all reason."

"Past all reason," Charlie echoed, pasting chicken salad onto his bread. There seemed to be a slight bluish mold on the edge of his top piece.

"When Earl was finally convinced and, more importantly, calmed down and gotten back on solid ground, Charlie proposed to him that both would say they had gotten me back safely to my house. I didn't stay under the Kohl dock as we had planned. That seemed a waste of time, so I got back on to the beach and walked home. But something wonderful, John, happened to me in that interval of swimming and walking. When I got back to the house, the place had changed. It seemed, really seemed, I'd come into someone else's place. All of my things were there, but it was as if I weren't there. I was only a visitor who had come to admire how Mrs. Peverill had acquired things and arranged them just so. And now where was Mrs. Peverill? Why couldn't she come to greet me? More significantly who was Mrs. Peverill, and was she really worth encountering? No, she seemed old and dated and utterly absent. We'd thought of it as a joke on Earl. I'd stay lost for a day or two just to see how that blow was taken on Longboat, but suddenly the prospect of never inhabiting old Mrs. Peverill, or finding a new shiny reality in some other universe was intoxicating. Absolutely intoxicating. It meant the whole life Harry and I had constructed didn't have to be the structure of our deaths. Didn't have to be the little engine we rode to the final collapsed bridge. I was giddy with that possibility. All of my things were no longer attached to me, it was like losing a tired skin, shedding a shell, bursting a cocoon, being pulled out of the crocodile's stomach. Running furiously at the wall and discovering as your toe touched it, that it melted into nothingness. It was like discovering the boiling pot simply wouldn't pour out any liquid. Of course, later I did want a few of my things."

"And all that was freeing?" Spradlin asked.

"Imagine you couldn't have, wouldn't have, asked that question. What would you be like if you couldn't fathom asking that question? What would you have to know to make such a question impossible?"

"I'd think you've put something in the chicken salad."

"That whole experience did put something in the chicken salad. What was it that could open a possible new life, an actual repudiation of everything you'd lived or thought or wanted or felt bruised about? That earlier, near-life led only to hurt joints, stooped back, and arthritic fingers, and grief over a partner who escaped early. You couldn't turn away from possibility. Here we were laughing over a joke on Earl and realizing the absolute freedom of what we were doing. Who'd want to go back? Who wouldn't want to steam ahead into a future unknowable, but reshape-able? Doesn't everybody want a second chance, maybe a third or a fourth? Who wouldn't want to get shut of foul entanglements?"

Spradlin was thinking, so Dyer is a better bet than dead Harry?

"No," she went on, "you don't have choices really, you just plunge ahead, rejecting the very notion of aspirations. You open yourself to experiences unencumbered with valuations. You simply are and awaiting the gorgeous unfolding."

"In a double-wide on the scummy backwaters of a polluted bay?" Spradlin said.

"That was a silly and harsh thing to say, John. I don't think it's you. I sense you already regret it, do you?" She stared at him and rather mechanically brought her paper napkin with its green balloons design to her lips.

"Yeah, maybe," Spradlin answered.

"Good! Then we can move on. I don't want to put you into Lem's class of pointless deal-making and acquisition galore, or Bainer's miracle-making in the midst of the rhetoric of salvation, or Noah's photographed lust, although I am jealous of Valery's utter delight in display, or the Russians' longing and hyper-patriotism and VanShuten's cunning use of that. They all think they can get what they want under the banner of saving or preserving Longboat Key. But of course, they'll all fail—"

"Lem's half way to Brazil right now," Dyer shouted.

"They'll all fail, won't they John? Because they'll all up in what they're doing, while Charlie and I have put all that away. Gotten shut of that. Gotten to clearer water by floating or swimming past those distractions, those little leavings of lost enterprises. New selves out of reach of those old possessions, old aspirations. Once you slide or swim past there's no return, not because it's impossible, but only because conceptualization of those concerns is no longer conjurable."

"Conjurable?"

"Beyond thought. It's like being alone in an infinite sea and gradually learning, interiorizing, that you are in fact a fish and at last at home."

"I'm not a fish, Tine, and neither are you. You owe some explanation to the people who cared about you, spent days and nights searching for you."

"Of course, I regret their efforts, although I might observe that might have been the most meaningful work of their lives. But Charlie and I are at the bottom of the sea and we cannot commune with people who live only to fly kites. We cannot see again their world, cannot breathe in it. Simply cannot. You cannot ask us."

"Okay. Okay. But shouldn't you at least say goodbye?"

"They've already said goodbye, haven't they? They've acknowledged death. What would be the lesson of reprieve? Just another chance to learn it all over again. How kind is that?"

"What about the legal issues?"

"Yes. Yes. Our point exactly. What about the legal issues? What about them? About them?"

Dyer said, half exalting, "Fish in a Kite world."

Spradlin smiled, nodded. "I'll do my part. Charlie, give me the keys now and when the time comes, I'll take the truck back to the store. I'll tell Jimmy you weren't feeling well. Pretty slow anyway. There's little or no work at the store, anyway."